DATE DUE

APR 2 3 2011		
JUN - 7 2011		
AUG 2 6 2011		
DEC 6 - 2011		
JAN 1 1 2012		
SEP 1 7 2012		
OCT 3 0 2012		
JAN - 8 2013		
07-29-15		

JOURNEY THROUGH FIRE

ALSO BY MAYA SNOW

Sisters of the Sword
Sisters of the Sword 2: Chasing the Secret

MAYA SNOW

Sisters of the Sword

JOURNEY THROUGH FIRE

HARPERCOLLINS*PUBLISHERS*

Journey Through Fire
Copyright © 2009 by Working Partners Limited
Series created by Working Partners Limited

Library of Congress Cataloging-in-Publication Data
Snow, Maya.
    Journey through fire / by Maya Snow.—1st ed.
        p.   cm.—(Sisters of the sword ; bk. 3)
    Summary: Recovering from injuries sustained while escaping a fire, Kimi,
Hana, along with their mother and little brother take refuge in a monastery
where their mother petitions the Shogun for gaining help against evil Uncle
Hidehira.
    ISBN 978-0-06-124393-6
    [1. Family problems—Fiction. 2. Brothers and sisters—Fiction. 3. Revenge—
Fiction. 4. Japan—History—1185–1600—Fiction.] I. Title.
    PZ7.S685115Jo 2009   2008032093
    [Fic]—dc22

Typography by Ray Shappell
09 10 11 12 13   CG/RRDB   10 9 8 7 6 5 4 3 2 1
❖
First Edition

To Amanda

ACKNOWLEDGMENTS

Special thanks to Karen Ball

Thanks also to Dr. Phillip Harries
of The Queen's College, Oxford,
for his invaluable advice and expertise.

Another thank you to Sensei John Jenkin of the
Koshinkan Aikido Society for the inspiration.

PROLOGUE

We had become a family without a home, creeping from place to place. Uncle Hidehira still roamed free, spreading death across the land. Our battle with him had forced us underground, and we had become prisoners hiding from the sun. We lived by the light of the moon now, moving under cover of darkness when one of our hideaways grew too dangerous. We were shadowless and invisible, like *oni* ghost spirits.

I could not have known it then, but that period in hiding sowed the seeds of something much worse than bloodshed. My family was reunited, but those days drove us apart, as we each found different ways of meeting the world that waited for us when we emerged.

My anger almost consumed me, and my struggle would leave Hana and me with scars we would carry forever. But in the end we found out just how strong our scars had made us.

We would need that strength like never before.

CHAPTER ONE

The battle raged around me. My hand went for the hilt of my sword but closed on empty space. Where was it? I staggered back as samurai soldiers swarmed past. Angry faces shouted curses from behind their kabuto helmets, and blood-smeared swords were raised against the blue sky. A horse galloped up. In the saddle sat an archer, his longbow held aloft. He looked down the shaft, pointing the arrowhead through the fighting crowds. As I watched, the soldier pulled back the strings and released an arrow. It sliced through the air, smooth and fluid. I twisted to watch its flight—and saw the face of our loyal friend, Tatsuya. No! I tried to cry out but no sound escaped me. Tatsuya's eyes opened wide in shock as the arrow found its home in his chest. He brought up a trembling hand and tried to yank out the arrow from between his ribs, but the shaft snapped in two. I wanted to help him, but it was too late.

A soldier in glittering samurai armor appeared and pushed my dying friend to the ground. The man and I gazed at each other across Tatsuya's bloody corpse. I recognized the eyes of *my uncle, staring back at me. His lip curled in a sneer.*

"It should have been you," he said, stepping over Tatsuya. And I knew his words were true. "Some say you're too young to die. But I say you're too dangerous to live."

I heard the hiss of metal as Uncle drew his sword and rested its point against my throat. The blade felt cool against my skin. Then with a single, rapid movement Uncle sliced my neck and blood ran down my chest, hot and sticky. My hands clutched at my throat, and I fell to my knees. I tried to cry out, but the only sound I could hear was the throaty laugh of my uncle as he watched my blood pool in the dirt.

"Good-bye, Kimi," he said. "It's time to join your father. . . ."

My eyes snapped open. I sat up sharply, my hands at my throat. Two hanging bamboo screens batted against each other, and a mosquito hovered in the air above me, droning. In a corner of the room a standing torch burned low.

I was nowhere near the battlefield. I was in the small village inn where I was hiding with my family. I didn't know whether to feel relief or regret as I sank back onto the thin mattress. I pulled the linen bed covering over my body.

Hana was lying on the floorboards beside me in the private room of the innkeeper, her face as peaceful as a baby's. Beyond her lay Mother and

Moriyasu. My little brother was curled up in the folds of Mother's robe.

We had escaped Uncle Hidehira and his samurai soldiers. But our freedom had come at a bitter price.

I turned my face to the wall and tried to erase the image from my nightmare of Tatsuya's lifeless eyes. He had been brave enough to stand shoulder to shoulder with us against Uncle in the past. But now our friend was gone, captured by faceless enemies— by ninja—and I didn't even know if he was still alive.

Hair stuck to my temples and my hands were clammy in the stuffy room. I felt a swelling of frustration in my chest. We should have been outside, helping the villagers with the early morning chores or riding around the estates raising an army! Instead, we dared not show our faces.

Beside me, Hana shifted in her sleep. I didn't want to wake her. *Enjoy your few moments of peace, sister,* I thought. *They'll be gone soon enough.* As if she'd heard my thoughts, Hana opened her eyes and gazed at me sleepily. She sat up and wrapped her slender arms around her legs.

"A new day," she said quietly. "I dreamed of Tatsuya again. He was helping us train like when we were at Master Goku's school."

I tried to smile, but my sister noticed how my expression faltered.

4

"What is it, Kimi?" Hana whispered, concerned. I had never been able to hide my feelings from her.

"I dreamed of him, too, Hana. But we weren't winning the fight."

Hana's brow furrowed.

"We have to get out of here," I whispered, flinging my covers to one side. I was struggling to breathe in the close heat of the room and tiptoed over to one of the joins in the screens where there was a gap just wide enough to see outside. I pushed my face to the crack. Whispers of sweet air brushed against my cheeks and I breathed in deeply.

"And do what?" my sister asked. She padded toward me on bare feet, careful not to make a noise. It wasn't just our sleeping mother and brother we had to think about. No one outside the inn could know we were here. I longed for the freedom that lay outside that door, but danger waited as well. Danger that felt closer by the day.

Suddenly a group of children ran past, calling out to one another. I drew back.

"Patience, Kimi," Hana said, keeping her voice low. "The innkeeper has risked his life to take care of us. We should be grateful."

A dandelion spore passed through the air between us and I tried to snatch it, but it glided out of my grasp, swimming away on an invisible current of air.

"I am grateful," I said, picking my words carefully, "but I am also tired of running! Enough hiding!"

Hana nodded, but she did not feel the same frustration I did at our situation. "The people of the villages certainly seem to be on our side." She looked up at me. "Can you believe it, Kimi? We have been on our own for so long and now . . . now, the people on the estates know our story. And they rebel against Uncle!"

It was true. While we had been hiding here, the innkeeper—Yoshiki—had brought us meals of rice and miso soup. Each day, as we shared this cramped space with him and his daughter, he would tell us stories of small defiance. There had been an early *Mushiokuri* ceremony in the fields for driving out pests, and the whisper had gone around the seed beds that the pest they were driving out was Hidehira.

"Only a few moon phases ago, no one would have dared question the *Jito*," Hana said.

The mood of the province was changing and for the first time the two of us could indulge in the luxury of hope. But menace still lurked; I could not relax my attention for a moment. Yoshiki also told us of how Uncle was rapidly tightening his grip and expanding his reach.

I looked past my sister at my sleeping brother and

mother. "We have our family back with us," I whispered, my throat tight with emotion.

Moriyasu rubbed his knuckles into his eyes, sighing. Mother turned in her sleep and draped a protective arm around her only surviving son.

"Soldiers! They're here!"

Yoshiki burst into the room, roughly sliding open the screen so that it made us jump. For these few days, he had been careful not to draw attention to us. Things had to be bad for him to be so reckless now.

He dropped to his knees in the center of the room and started to pull up floorboards. His face was red and shiny with sweat. Understanding the danger, I threw myself to the ground and grappled with a board, heaving until it gave way.

"Are you sure?" I asked.

"They're looking for you, I think," he said. "There's no other reason they would have come back." Our eyes locked. We both knew that this was life or death. And not only for my family and me. Yoshiki and the whole village could be killed if we were discovered.

"Thank you," I said.

Yoshiki nodded and glanced at Moriyasu. Our brother had been woken by the disturbance and was watching us keenly. Mother stirred behind him. I realized that Yoshiki shared our hopes—that one day

Moriyasu, our father's rightful heir, would grow up to return these estates to stability and happiness.

"Don't thank me," Yoshiki said, turning back. "Just try to stay alive."

Mother and Moriyasu scrambled to their feet. Mother's hands trembled as she pulled her robe tight around her waist and accepted the sword that Yoshiki held out to her. Little Moriyasu bit his lip, trying not to show his fear. Our father's son, he had been brave for so long.

"I usually store rice down here, but there's none left," Yoshiki explained. "It will make a good hiding place for you."

Outside, we could hear screams and cries for help among terse voices issuing commands. Looking out through the main room, I saw a woman dragged past the open screen by a samurài soldier. The thick leather panels of his armor glistened in the sunlight and the bronze trim on his iron helmet shone dangerously. If he had turned his head, he would have seen us.

There was no time to waste.

I scrambled into the shallow dirt cavity and reached for my sister, pulling her down beside me. Moriyasu leaped in next to us. Mother gracefully stepped down, Yoshiki holding her hand to steady her. Even in this danger, her face remained serene.

"Stay calm, my children," she said, lying on the packed earth beside us.

"Good luck to you," Yoshiki whispered. Then the wooden floorboards were put back in place over our heads.

It felt as though we were being buried alive.

I stared up at the dark floorboards. My arms were pinned to my sides by the bodies of my sister and brother and the air was thick with the scent of wood, so close to our faces. Yoshiki threw a mat over where we were hiding and dust settled onto us. My eyes itched with grit, forcing slow tears to streak down either side of my face. I couldn't move to wipe them away. I licked my lips nervously and immediately regretted it as dirt filled my mouth. *Stay strong,* I willed myself. I could feel Hana's fingers twitching beside me as she struggled to control her own panic. Moriyasu let out a quiet sob.

"Sit there, my sweet one," I heard Yoshiki say gently above. "Try not to move."

"Why?" a small voice asked. It was Sakura, Yoshiki's daughter. The innkeeper was using his own daughter as a decoy. We heard the floorboards shift as Sakura came to take her place on the mat above our heads. I whispered a silent prayer of thanks and promised myself that one day I would repay this innocent girl, caught in the chase.

Heavy footsteps sounded nearby—confident, aggressive, and determined. Fate had arrived at our doorway. I twisted my wrist so that my fingertips could brush against the back of Hana's hand.

"Are you the innkeeper?" a deep voice demanded. I heard Yoshiki fall to his knees in front of the man. I could just see Yoshiki's flushed face through a crack between the floorboards that weren't covered by the mat.

"I am," he acknowledged.

"Ten bags of rice from each village are to be bestowed upon the esteemed Lord Steward Yamamoto, now that he controls these lands. Hand over your rice immediately."

"I am sorry, sir, but I have nothing for you. All our rice has long gone to the Lord Steward. We are destitute." I admired Yoshiki for the calmness of his speech. The soldier would almost certainly have his hand on his sword.

"I don't believe you!" shouted the soldier, enraged.

A sudden scuffling sound made me catch my breath.

"Father!" Sakura cried out above us.

Yoshiki's feet dragged on the floorboards as he was pulled across the room.

"Show me your supplies!" I could imagine the

spittle landing on Yoshiki's cheeks. Yoshiki was thrown out of the little room, footsteps following him.

Silence fell, though I could hear my heart pumping hard in my chest. I waited for a movement from Sakura; for her to run after her father. She shifted her weight uneasily above us, but stayed put.

"Father?" she whispered into the empty room, and her small voice broke and trembled. I wished I could put my arms around her and comfort her. But there was no comfort to be had for any of us.

All we could do was wait.

CHAPTER TWO

I could hear my brother whispering a prayer as we waited. A bead of sweat ran down my temple and into my ear. But there was no more sign of the soldiers. Perhaps we had been lucky. Perhaps a divine wind had saved us from a brush with Uncle's samurai. I dared to breathe a sigh of relief.

Then the door screens were ripped down and Moriyasu jumped beside me. My own back went rigid as I tried to control the emotions that flooded me.

Men ran into the room and I heard Sakura cry out as the table in the corner was turned over and clay pots slammed against the walls. I could imagine how easily the modest furniture was being smashed to pieces. Our home for these few days was being obliterated.

"Pull this place to pieces!" a deep voice ordered. "These people will not hide anything from us. Get the girl out of the way!"

Feet paced across the floor.

"Please, no! I beg you; do not harm my daughter."

Yoshiki's words rang out. He'd forgotten to keep his voice low and respectful. There was a dull thud and a small cry as thick leather smacked against small ribs—then a crash. I knew that Sakura had been kicked into something above us.

I bit my lip hard to stop myself from shouting out in anger. The iron tang of blood filled my mouth. I could not stand that we were the reason for all of this suffering. I heard Yoshiki being dragged across the room and then could see him being hurled to the floor.

"Stay out of our way," someone said, before spitting on the floor beside him. Yoshiki's humiliation was complete and it was all our fault. He turned his face and his eyes met mine through the sliver of space that had become my window on the world. His gaze remained steady for a moment, then he turned his face to the floor and whispered a prayer for mercy.

"Look!" someone cried out. "The fool's given away his hiding place. He was looking over there!" Heavy feet stomped over, then the mat was tossed aside and the rickety floorboards above our faces shuddered and bounced on the joists.

"No, you misunderstand," Yoshiki tried to protest. "There is nothing here; I promise you." I could hear the desperation in his voice. So could the soldiers. Someone paced across the room and slapped a hand across Yoshiki's face, making him cry out in pain. I hoped that the innkeeper would say nothing more. He was in danger of being killed.

Dirt rained down on us as a soldier grappled with the corner of a floorboard and I heard his gasp of satisfaction as the board came up and he threw it to one side.

He thrust his face into the space beside us. The man squinted and blinked. We had become accustomed to the musty dark that surrounded us, but after the bright midday sun, this samurai could see nothing. Blindly he thrust a hand into the cavity, grasping at the empty space. His calloused hands felt the air in front of my face, and I pressed my lips together. I could not let him feel even the whisper of my breath on his fingertips.

Impatiently he reared back and tore at a second floorboard. I held my palms flat against my thighs and pressed down, hoping that the pressure would stop my trembling. I could hear Mother whispering a reassurance to Moriyasu. Beside me, Hana continued to stare straight up, her eyes unwavering.

The second floorboard broke in two as it gave way. The soldier's head and shoulders lunged down, but this time he had shifted his position and faced away from us. He craned his head around, coughing and spluttering.

"The rice must be here somewhere," he grunted.

"Enough!" roared the same voice we had heard before. I guessed this was the captain of the samurai. "There's nothing here. We'll tear this village apart, and take the children, too. They will make fine recruits for the *Jito*'s army."

The samurai acknowledged the order and footsteps thudded out of the inn.

I gasped. I felt my blood heat up. Hana guessed at my emotions and reached out to take my hand. I had already seen my own family torn apart; I could not let them do this.

Then came the sound of Sakura gasping in pain, and Yoshiki pleading again. I heard a dragging sound and could clearly picture the poor little girl being pulled along by her hair. My anger was hotter than fire by now.

"You say you have nothing for us?" bellowed the samurai. Silence fell, sliced by the sound of sword sliding out of its scabbard. "Bid your little girl farewell, innkeeper!"

"No!" I cried, tearing my hand out of Hana's.

Above us, everything went silent. "What's that?" asked the voice of the captain.

"No, Kimi! I beg you!" Mother hissed at me. But I closed my mind to her voice. I leaped out of our shallow grave, landing in a sideways stance, hands up. I had no weapons, but I had my spirit.

15

The samurai captain's eyes shone with eagerness to fight. He was many hands taller than me. He tossed Sakura aside, and the little girl scrambled over to her father; then the samurai set his feet wide apart as he faced me.

"You!" said the samurai. The innkeeper was right; they had come back for us.

I jumped to the side and reached out, grasping one of the broken floorboards. I swung it low and knocked his feet out from under him. The captain sprawled on the floor. He looked up and his face was twisted with anger.

"You little fool," he spat. "Do you think you can take me on?" He called out to his men as he picked himself up off the floor. But I could see he was off balance. I kicked him hard in the chest and he fell again. A sense of victory coursed through me, though I knew the fight wasn't over yet.

Behind me, I could hear Mother, Hana, and my brother scrabbling out of our hiding place. I looked over my shoulder to see my family standing in a row, ready to fight. Even Moriyasu. Yoshiki gently put his daughter down—and then sprang to his feet, just as a soldier ran into the room.

"Aaiii!" My mother's voice rang out as she darted past me and swung her sword's blade through the gut of the soldier, using a strength I didn't know she had. He fell heavily to the floor, his eyes rolling back in his head. Yoshiki raced to relieve the dead soldier of his sword.

Three more samurai rushed into the room. They hesitated, shocked at the sight of their dead friend.

"Get them!" shouted the captain, struggling to get up. "Do whatever it takes."

But before the last words left his mouth, my family was upon them. My mother sent a swift kick into the face of one of the soldiers. Blood shot out of his nostrils and his face contorted in pain and surprise.

Hana turned on her right heel and kicked out her left foot as straight as an arrow into the stomach of another soldier. With the air knocked out of him, he staggered to one side. Moriyasu delivered a swift push to knock him to the ground.

The third samurai lunged toward Yoshiki.

"Father!" a warning voice called out. It was Sakura.

But Yoshiki had already spotted the soldier coming for him. "Get back!" Yoshiki called out to Sakura. She scrambled behind an overturned table. Yoshiki raised his sword high above his head and swung it around to bring the blade across the man's cheek, scoring the flesh so that his face poured blood.

The samurai captain was back on his feet, and he threw himself at me. I stepped slightly to the side, and his hand moved the air in front of my face. But he was fast and struck out again with his other hand, knocking me against the wall and into the standing torch.

It clattered to the floor. The tinder-dry mats caught immediately. Flames were soon licking up the walls of the inn. The fire showed my sister's face in a golden light that looked almost beautiful—until I smelled the smoke. Shreds of flaming straw fell down on my head, and I realized the straw roof was alight. I brushed them away frantically, dreading that my hair might catch like the straw.

"Get out!" I called to Hana, but a samurai was behind her. The breath caught in my throat as I saw the long arc of his sword glisten in the light of the fire; he was about to kill her.

"No!" Yoshiki rushed under the raised blade, grabbed the hilt of the sword, and twisted, until the soldier's wrists threatened to snap. The sword clattered to the ground. The soldier fell to his knees, as the choking smoke swirled around him. The raging fire threatened to consume us.

"Kimi!" Yoshiki called to me. "Get out of here!" A wall of fire had appeared between us. Yoshiki pushed Moriyasu closer to the open door of the inn and my brother raced toward the only way out. Then Yoshiki grabbed the hands of Hana and my mother and they followed, crouching low to avoid the heavy clouds of smoke. Yoshiki glanced back only once, past the narrow trail of fire that divided me from the others. "Get Sakura! Please!" he called to me.

Sakura! I had almost forgotten. My eyes were streaming and my lungs felt as though embers of fire were burning inside them. I swiveled around and spotted what looked like a crushed pile of clothes in the corner. Sakura! I threw myself to the floor and crawled on my hands and knees toward Sakura, the little girl who had never asked to become involved in my battle. Now I could see her face, the huge eyes shut tight in pain and the shallow rise and fall of her chest. She was smeared with soot and a small flame threatened to catch her dress.

Choking and gasping for breath, I reached her. Gently I lifted her in my arms. She weighed less than the cherry blossom she had been named after. But as I turned to escape, a burning rafter fell from the roof of the inn. I leaped out of the way and took a step toward the door, but suddenly the samurai captain, sword in hand, stepped into my path, ignoring the angry tide of flames around us. From the expression on his face, I knew exactly what this man wanted.

My blood on his blade.

CHAPTER THREE

Prepare to die," the soldier hissed. Rivers of sweat poured down his cheeks but he stood his ground, as the hungry flames crawled up the walls of the hut.

"Captain! Where are you?" shouted the voices of his soldiers outside. He did not call back, and his gaze never faltered as he took a step closer.

Sakura shifted in my arms and burrowed her face into the crook of my neck. Loosening her grip from my shoulders, I quickly lowered her to the floor.

"Run, Sakura," I whispered in her ear. I turned her around toward the open door and gave her a shove. She broke into a run toward the open doorway. The captain did not even glance down at her. She was small enough to duck past the worst of the flames and low enough to the ground not to choke on the smoke. I watched her hair bounce against her shoulders and felt my heart squeeze tight as she raced from the room.

The captain's gaze never left my face. As he stepped toward me, I looked around frantically and spotted a discarded sword lying on the floor. I reached across the searing heat and grabbed it.

Then I ran toward my enemy, forcing myself not to think about the flames that clawed at me. I brought the sword around in a smooth arc, slicing through fire and smoke. The soldier lifted his own sword to deflect my attack. The point of my sword uselessly pierced a wooden floorboard. I heaved to release it but my opponent was already bringing his blade toward my ribs. Instinctively I dropped to the floor and rolled out of the way, across the burning floorboards.

I sprang to my feet, unarmed once more, and patted away the few flames that had caught at the hem of my tunic. I was dimly aware of the sweat that poured down my back and the tears streaming from my eyes. The smoke and heat were oppressive, and the hut groaned and popped as its wooden frame burned. I had to get out of here—fast. But the soldier stood between me and the door of the hut. The panels of his armor caught the orange light of the flames as he raised his sword high over his head.

"I shall cut you into eight pieces," he said.

Like Kagutsuchi, the god of fire, I thought.

But before he could make his move, a cloud of smoke drifted past him. He doubled over in a coughing fit. When he straightened up, tears were running down his cheeks and he drew the back of his hand across his face. The sweat on his throat glistened.

I didn't hesitate.

I yanked my sword from the wooden board and swung it around to slash the soldier's waist between the ties of his armor. A gasp escaped his lips as his sword clattered to the floor. He gripped his stomach, blood spurting out between his fingers.

With one swift movement I raised my sword above my head. Then I brought it around and sliced through his throat. As I watched, his body fell slowly forward, into the flames. Fire danced up around him and I turned away.

Now I had to escape.

I cast my sword aside and tried to wave the smoke away with my hands. My lungs felt as though they were burning and I could not stop coughing and retching from the smoke. The heat of the flames burned my cheeks. I staggered against a timber post but leaped away again as the touch of the burning wood seared my skin.

"Help!" I cried out, stumbling toward what I thought could be the doorway but soon realized was just another burning wall. It was impossible to hear if anyone called back an answer, as the crackle of flames had filled my ears. I tried to cry out again, but my throat burned as soon as I opened my mouth.

Despair flooded through me and my legs went weak. I crumpled onto the floor grabbing at my throat, trying to pull the neckline of my tunic loose in the hope that I might breathe more easily. My vision started to blur.

I was defeated.

As I lay on the floor I pulled my knees toward my chest and watched the flames. I was surrounded by a curtain of fire that was drawing ever closer. I thought of my mother, picturing her kind face. Tears rolled down my cheeks, cool against the heat. "Keep my brother safe," I whispered into the parched air. "Let him finish what Hana and I began."

I closed my eyes as the fire came to consume me.

Thwack! From behind me, I heard the sound of wood splintering. A hole had appeared in the fiery wall of the hut, through which precious tendrils of fresh air unfurled. Flames jumped up eagerly, fed by the air. I tried to reach out toward the gap in the wall, but I was too weak.

A hand reached in and grabbed hold of my tunic, pulling fiercely. The hem of the cloth, charred by the fire, tore away. Then the hand grabbed again, hooking under my armpit. A shard of wood was angrily pulled away and then another hand came through, hooking under my other side. My rescuer dragged me toward the small opening.

Whoosh! There was a flash of angry yellow, as the hut was consumed by a massive fireball. The fresh air had brought life back to my lungs—but it had given the fire more life, too. Searing pain flooded my head and an acrid, singed smell filled my nostrils. My scalp felt as though it had been plunged into boiling tar. I could hear voices now. The noise and the pain overran my senses until I could stand no more.

My eyes slowly shut and my mind cleared.

It was a relief to leave this place.

I opened my eyes and found myself surrounded by darkness. I felt the cool touch of linen covers against my skin. I tried to raise myself up on my elbows but a restraining hand gently pushed me back down to the mattress. I didn't resist; every muscle in my body screamed with the effort of moving.

"Am I a prisoner?" I asked, wondering if my rescuer was one of Uncle's samurai. I blinked several times as my eyes slowly focused on a man's face. Brown eyes with green flecks in them. Smiling kindly, he reached out a hand to smooth away the frown that creased my brow. His touch was feather light.

"You're safe," he said, pulling the covers tighter

around my shoulders. "Now sleep."

"What about Hana? Where is she?" I asked. The monk shook his head.

"Now is not the time to talk." As he walked away I felt my vision blur again. Sleep descended and I surrendered to it.

I slowly opened my eyes. Weak light flooded the room. I moved my limbs beneath the covers, testing to see how much my body still hurt. I could feel scabs on my back catching against the cover, and my head was filled with a dull, insistent throb. Ignoring the pain, I turned my head to look around the room.

In the corner stood a pile of bed linen; bottles of fluids were half hidden behind a *byobu* screen. Beyond the paper screen was another mattress with a small boy sitting cross-legged. I frowned as I tried to focus on him. Then I recognized the familiar face, watching me keenly.

"Moriyasu!" I said. He leaped to his feet and ran over to me, throwing himself into my arms. His embrace made me wince in pain, but the relief I felt that my brother had made it out alive was instant medicine. I quickly wiped my eyes free of tears as he pulled back to look at me.

"You're awake," he said. His gaze wandered over my face and I noticed a frown start to form, but before

I could ask him what was wrong, he shook himself. "Aren't you hungry?"

My stomach did feel hollow.

"How long has it been?" I asked.

"Too long," Moriyasu said. "I've been lonely without you." I tried to smile, but the skin of my face stretched tight. I lifted a hand to my temples, but Moriyasu quickly grabbed my fingers and entwined them with his own.

"Hurrah!" he said. "Someone to tease again. I have a lot of teasing to catch up on."

I pushed him away gently. My brother was trying to distract me. But why?

"Help me get up," I said, sitting up in bed. Moriyasu looked uncertain.

"You've been very ill, Kimi," he said. "The monks have been looking after you." A pair of kind eyes surfaced in my memory.

"I remember," I said. Then I realized that Mother and Hana were missing. "The others?" I asked him, not daring to say my worst fears out loud.

My brother brought his hands together in a small prayer of thanks. "They're both safe. At least . . ." I reached out, despite the pain that shot down my back, and pulled Moriyasu toward me.

"Please tell me," I said.

Moriyasu looked up into my face. "Hana is being

looked after by the monks, too." He paused and his gaze fell to the tiled floor.

"I must go to her," I said. "Take me." Moriyasu glanced at an indigo silk robe that hung on the door, brought it to me, and helped me up. I felt weak, but I was determined. I straightened up, and could feel the cuts and scrapes shifting painfully on my back. I looked down at myself and could not see any burns; I had been lucky.

Moriyasu led the way as I took small, faltering steps across the room. My head throbbed, rushing rivers of pain that fell all the way down the back of my neck; I felt as though, at any moment, I would crumble to the floor like an empty shroud.

But I had to be strong. I had to see my sister.

We passed the ointments and potions of the sick room and the large bowl of water caught my eye. The bottom of the black slate bowl was carved with a phoenix stretching his huge wings. The bird of fire. But I knew that, in legends, this bird also represented the start of something new. Then, in the reflection of the water, as glossy and smooth as a dawn lake—the image of a face. The skin around the eyes was young and unlined, yet the eyes looked as though they had seen too much. Above them was a smooth forehead.

Looking closer I could see tufts of hair sticking

out at odd angles and skin puckering at the temples. I turned my head to look more closely and the reflection shifted.

My heart thudded in my chest. "It cannot be," I said in a whisper.

CHAPTER FOUR

I let Moriyasu's hand fall and lifted my fingers to my head. The ghost in the water did the same. I reached out to my reflection, drawing closer until my fingers touched the surface, destroying the image. I ran my hands over my head. My hair—gone! Images flooded my mind as I recalled the heat of the fire that chased me. I remembered being dragged out of the hut and how my head had felt ravaged by the molten hatred of the fire. My body did not burn, but my hair did.

My hands fell to my sides. I felt numb—unable to cry. I turned around and looked at Moriyasu. His lip trembled as he met my glance. I turned away sharply.

"Don't look at me," I said, as I brought my hands over my face. I heard Moriyasu walk toward me, and then he gently drew my hands away until he was looking at me steadily, without judgment or disgust. But I knew I looked hideous.

"I don't know what I'm going to do," I said, as I turned back to the doorway. "At least when I had long hair I could tie it up and disguise myself as a boy. How do I disguise my bare head? I look like a priest—or a beggar!" I tried to laugh, but it didn't come easily.

Moriyasu took my hand again. "It doesn't matter, Kimi," he said simply. "You're alive."

The scent of burning incense filled my nostrils as I stood on the threshold of the room where my sister lay. A futon was surrounded by linen drapes that billowed in the breeze from an open window. It was as if the bed were floating.

A drape was pulled aside and someone moved away from the side of the bed. It was a monk. He carried a bowl of water with flower petals floating on the surface. Beyond him I could see Hana's profile. Her lips were parted slightly as her chest rose and fell. Her skin looked as white as a crane's feathers.

"Hana!" I whispered and ran forward. The monk stepped neatly to one side as I pushed past him. I was so worried about my sister that I didn't stop to think about the disrespect I was showing. I kneeled at Hana's bedside, searching her face for signs of pain. But her expression was serene. I looked at the monk, wanting some answers.

Gently he lowered himself until he was kneeling by my side. "My name is Daisuke," the monk began. I bowed my head in greeting and he did the same, before turning back to my sister. "She is sleeping," he said. "A very deep sleep." His gaze remained fixed on my sister's face. He reached out a hand and drew a thumb across her forehead. I didn't know what it meant, but I could feel the sincerity and warmth that came from this young man. He could only be good for Hana.

I leaned back and allowed my head to bow. "What happened to her?" I asked, watching my hands twist and knot in my lap. Daisuke turned to me.

"She has been through a great deal," he said. "And so have you."

Then he put a hand under my chin, lifting my head so that I was forced to meet his gaze. I recognized the flashes of green among the brown of his eyes—eyes as deep as the lake I'd rowed across to find my mother. This was the man I'd seen when I'd woken from my own illness.

His gaze rose to my scalp, and when it did, I felt the burning sensation return—as if the ravaged skin knew it was being examined and was protesting. I knew what it looked like. My imagination traced the pattern of burns, the taut skin, and red, angry flesh. I must have looked so ugly to him. He turned my chin to one side and then the other as he inspected my injuries. I felt my cheeks flush with shame as I tried not to pull away.

"Healing well," he commented. "As for Hana, your sister has suffered a great trauma," he continued. "You remember the fire?"

How could I forget? "But I don't understand," I said. "Hana got out to safety. I was the last one in the burning inn."

Daisuke's face turned serious. "Your sister returned, Kimi," he explained. "She reached into the fire to pull you out. Now she must take the time to recover from her bravery. Strong actions ask much of the body and mind. She needs time and medicine to heal herself."

I looked back at Hana. A flash of memory returned, and I saw the hand reaching through the flames to grab me. My glance fell to the bandages around my sister's arm and understanding dawned. I tried to swallow, but my throat felt dry. While she tried to grip me, reaching in through the burning wooden wall, her arms spent too long in the flames.

"What have I done?" I whispered.

The monk inclined his head. "Her burned skin will heal. You must be grateful to her, Kimi. Do not turn gratitude into guilt. That serves no one. Your sister must love you very much. Cherish that love."

I got to my feet and sat on the side of the bed. I pulled one of Hana's hands into my lap and turned it over to trace the pattern of lines on her palm, unscathed by the fire. My vision blurred as I thought about the fire. I saw again the samurai captain's face twisting in a sneer. I recalled the sight of the rising flames . . . remembered thinking that I was not going to escape the inn alive. My fingers tightened around my sister's hand.

"Forgive me," I said. I could see Hana's eyes move beneath her eyelids and her hand twitched in mine. "Did she hear me?" I asked, turning around to search the monk's face.

He shook his head, regretfully. "She's dreaming," he explained. "For now, your sister is far away from you."

I got to my feet and went to gaze out of the window at the bright red leaves of a maple tree. My sister had never been away from me before. The thought of it made my heart sing with despair.

I wiped the tears that streaked my cheeks and told myself that I had to stay strong—for Hana.

I turned back to the room. Daisuke was holding a long-handled pan over the red coals of a fire that burned in a corner. In the pan I could see a scattering of long, green *biwa* leaves. Curiosity drew me to the monk's side.

"What are you doing?" I asked.

"I practice *kanpo*—herbal medicine," Daisuke explained. "I help heal visitors to the monastery under the tutelage of the *kanpo* master."

The scent of the roasting *biwa* leaves filled the room as he carefully tipped them into a mortar and added a few drops of oil. He threw in a handful of *nazuna* white flower heads. Even I recognized this plant—it grew all over the countryside.

"I know those plants!" I said. "They help with healing, don't they?" Daisuke nodded. "When we were children, my sister and I would use them to heal pretend wounds when we were out playing in the woods."

"I'm impressed," he said. "I've traveled to many places and studied with many teachers to learn my craft, but you've been taught the same lessons at home." For the first time, I wondered if this monk knew who I was—who my family were. Did these men know that they were giving shelter to a set of people my uncle—the *Jito*—would do anything to have slaughtered? Did these monks understand the risk they were taking?

"Do not worry," Daisuke said as he offered me the pestle. Was he talking about Hana or could he tell what I was thinking? But something in his voice convinced me that I should listen.

I sat on the mat to begin pounding. It felt good to grind the leaves into a paste—to help my sister. When Daisuke indicated that it was ready, I took the pestle and mortar over to Hana's bedside. Daisuke stood beside me and massaged the ends of my sister's fingers. I watched as he narrowed his eyes, concentrating hard.

"Her heart is growing stronger," he said. "She's ready." He paused and looked at me carefully. "Are you?" I nodded, even though I barely understood what Daisuke was asking me.

He pulled back my sister's sheets and slowly, carefully removed the bandage to reveal her arm.

"No!" I gasped, stumbling backward. My sister's skin glistened with yellow pus. Shreds of dead skin had torn away, where they'd dried and stuck to the sheets. Angry blisters were scattered across her right arm and her beautiful ivory skin had been burned to a dull red, puckering at the edges of the wounds. The room started to swirl and Daisuke waved a hand before my face, encouraging me to close my eyes. I closed them tight and let the darkness take over. At Daisuke's command, I breathed in and out once, twice, trying to clear my mind. When I opened my eyes again, the room stayed still. *Be strong,* I reminded myself. *Tears can come later. I have to help.*

I kneeled at Hana's bedside again, grateful that it

was just this one arm that was burned, and scooped a handful of the green poultice out of the mortar. Daisuke showed me how to apply it to my sister's skin. Whispering a prayer, I pressed the pungent green leaves against my sister's arm. I looked anxiously at her face, but I didn't seem to be causing her any pain. Daisuke passed me a roll of linen strips.

"Bind the poultice to her skin," he said. "She will heal more quickly."

Reverentially I bandaged my sister. Her arm felt as light as air as I lifted it off the bed to wind the bandages. I placed her hand back on the mattress by her side.

My task was done. I pulled my hands together in front of me and allowed my head to sink onto my chest. The sound of sobbing filled the room. With a moment's shock, I realized it was my own cries that rang in my ears.

Suddenly Daisuke was by my side.

"She's alive, Kimi," he said. "For that, count your blessings."

My blessings . . . As I gazed back at my sister, memories flooded my mind. I remembered the way Hana and I had chased each other through fields as children, her quiet support when we were disguised as boys—even her fierce fight by my side in the bloody battle against our uncle's soldiers. My blessings were many, and they were all entwined around the figure of my sister. And now Hana lay, peaceful—how could I deny her this chance to rest, after all that had happened to us? Motes of dust danced in the air above her and the drapes around her bed shifted easily in the breeze. She was safe; that's all I needed to know. For now, there was nothing more I could do.

CHAPTER FIVE

K imi!"
I swiveled around. Mother stood in the
doorway and I ran to her. The wide sleeves
of her robe swung around my shoulders as she drew
me to her in a rare embrace. I could smell a hint of
plum in her hair. Eventually she drew back.

I watched my mother's gaze falter as her eyes were
drawn toward my naked head with its burns and
scars.

"Oh, Kimi," she said, sadness flooding her eyes.

"It's nothing," I said, wanting her to stop staring.
"Skin heals and hair grows back." I hoped I sounded
braver than I felt.

"And in the meantime . . ." Mother pulled a
sheath of silk from her sash. It was midnight blue,
with dots of pure white running through it, like
stars in the sky. Mother took the silk and turned
me around.

"Silk is cool against the skin," she explained, as

she wrapped the square around my head. "If you tuck this corner in here, twist the other corner, and tie it here—"

When she'd finished, she placed her hands on my shoulders. "No one would ever know," she said.

I felt a pang of anguish at the hopeful determination in her voice. *Is Mother ashamed of me?* I wondered. But I shook myself. She loved me; she was upset.

"You were very brave in the fire," Mother said, as Moriyasu sat on the edge of Hana's mattress. He took Hana's hand and kneaded the palm, encouraging the circulation as Daisuke had done.

Mother's voice drew my gaze back to her. "But you played a dangerous game."

"What do you mean?" I asked, unable to stop my eyes drifting to the floor. Of course, I could guess what she meant. She put a hand beneath my chin and lifted my head until I was forced to look her in the eye.

"I have lost a husband and two sons," she said quietly. "I do not wish to lose my daughters, too."

"I'm sorry," I said uselessly. I wanted to save Sakura, but I never meant any harm to befall my beloved sister.

Suddenly the clouds of incense in the room became overpowering. I had to get out of here— had to find fresh air. I looked around the room. "I need to . . ." Before I could finish speaking, Daisuke arrived at my side.

"Shall I show you around the monastery?" he asked calmly. Relief replaced the panic in me. He looked at Mother and Moriyasu. "Please. Come with us. Hana must rest."

With a farewell glance in Hana's direction, I stepped out of the room, my mother and brother following. One side of the walkway opened up onto a serene rock garden. The buildings were arranged around the garden in a U-shape, and through the opening I could see outside to the main gate of the monastery.

"This building is where the monks live," Daisuke said. "The temple and formal gardens are farther back in the compound."

Monks moved quietly along the corridors, carrying piles of linen towels. Each monk had his head closely shaved to show his commitment to the holy life.

"Is it hard work?" I asked Daisuke as Mother hurried forward to catch up to Moriyasu, who was pretending to sword fight up ahead. "To live a holy life?" I had never had the chance to ask this of anyone before and I hoped that the monk would not be insulted by my questions. But he was only a few years older than I—his skin was still fresh and unlined—and perhaps he would not mind talking to me.

"It is hard work to attain a state of peace in one's mind, to let go of selfish needs. I learned not to get attached to things in this world a long time ago," he began. Then he hesitated and smiled. "That's not quite right," he admitted. "I'm still learning not to be prideful, to let go. It is a daily duel within myself, but I believe that many inspiring things can happen if one can attain the right perspective on life. If one can learn to accept that there is much more than just what we can see and hear . . . what we can touch."

I gazed back down at the monks moving around us. These were men who had chosen to turn their backs on a life of personal vanity; surely with my burns I could do the same. Then Daisuke surprised me. "These are warrior monks, Kimi," he continued. "They would risk anything in the fight for their beliefs." I looked again and noticed the heavy sashes that the men wore, perfect for carrying swords. Some even carried bamboo and rattan bows.

"What are you saying?" I asked. Daisuke stretched out an arm and indicated toward the green mountains that reared up beyond the monastery.

"Word of your struggle has traveled the countryside," he said in a low voice. I looked up, startled. These monks knew all about Hana and me. They knew we had been fighting Uncle and that we were a danger to their monastery—why were they being so good to us?

But I didn't have a chance to ask; Daisuke's eyes hardened as his voice turned serious. "Are you willing to reach for the highest height? To win the battle within yourself and let go of the emotions that will destroy you from the inside?"

I didn't know what he meant. I was willing to fight any battle—but one against myself? "I don't know," I admitted.

"Then you need to decide," Daisuke said to me. "You have encountered much and are about to face even more. What will carry you through is the flame in your heart. If it burns for vengeance, you will consume yourself in the fire. But if it is the cherished flame of love, then it will light your way. Only you can choose which flame."

I was stunned. He barely knew me, and yet he knew how brightly my passion for revenge burned. But why should I struggle against it? "But without vengeance, how can—"

Just then, Moriyasu ran back to us and tugged on the hem of Daisuke's sleeve. "Daisuke! Let's play tag!" he pleaded, his face shining with joy. Then he raced away down the walkway toward the gardens, his voice echoing off the smooth wooden floors as he called out excitedly.

Daisuke gave me a small bow, a smile playing on his lips. "Excuse me," he said—then he broke into a run, chasing my little brother into the garden.

I thought about what he'd said. I did have love in my heart, but I had hatred and anger for my uncle, too. Surely both things would help me in my mission to bring down my enemy.

Mother fell into step beside me and smiled, watching the monk and our brother play. The long folds of her robe swept the floor as she took delicate steps. She remained silent, occasionally bowing her head to acknowledge passing servants.

"The innkeeper rescued us," she said eventually. She peered into my face to see if I was ready. I nodded in acknowledgment. I needed to hear what had happened after I'd been rescued from the fire.

"Yoshiki," I murmured. "But the village was crawling with Uncle's samurai. How did he get us out?"

"He was quick," Mother said. She slashed a hand through the air. "While the soldiers were still turning huts inside out, he loaded us all onto his packhorses. Thankfully you had passed out and could no longer feel any pain. The journey was not an easy one." Mother stopped talking, and I could see that she was struggling to contain her emotions. I waited a moment before asking the next question.

"And what of Yoshiki and the villagers?" A new,

dreadful thought struck me. "What of Sakura?" I demanded, my mouth suddenly dry. The last I saw of the innkeeper's daughter, she was running toward the exit. I prayed to the gods that she was still alive. I could not bear it if a child had died because of me.

"Fear not," Mother told me. "The villagers escaped to neighboring villages. Despite your uncle's best efforts, the people of this land still flourish. And a certain little girl is still playing happily in the fields." A sob caught in my throat. Up ahead, my little brother cried out in delight as Daisuke swept him up off the gravel and balanced him on his shoulders.

"And are *we* safe?" I asked, watching my brother and thinking of my sister, lying in her bed. Uncle had been attacking villages so aggressively over the past few weeks. I wasn't sure that anywhere could be safe.

"For now," Mother reassured me. "Even your uncle would not dare attack warrior monks. We are lucky. Your father visited this monastery several times and the monks here are sympathetic to Moriyasu's claim. But they will not enter violent conflict unless circumstances are extreme. They aim only to keep us safe from harm."

"Come," Daisuke said, lowering Moriyasu from his shoulders as he returned to us. "It is time to eat." The mere mention of food made my head spin.

We walked into an open room with sliding panels and a low wooden table. In one corner was a *tokonoma*, an alcove with a hanging scroll. In the alcove was a golden board made of Kaya wood, on which a black grid was painted. Smooth black and white pebbles sat in bowls beside the board.

"What's that?" I asked, as my little brother took my hand and led me toward the dining table.

Moriyasu laughed. "You'll find out," he said mysteriously, "when I beat you! It's a game called Go that comes from China. Daisuke taught me how to play it. He can teach you, if you like. But you have to be very *clever* to play it. I'm not sure . . ." He shook his head gravely, as if uncertain of my abilities, but he could not contain his giggles.

"Hmm, it seems both of us need to be taught a lesson," I said, squeezing his hand and smiling. It was good to see my brother laughing and teasing. I allowed myself to hope that the horrors of the past moons had not left a permanent scar on his heart.

My family and I took our places at the table while Daisuke excused himself. He soon returned with a tray of food, and my mouth watered at the sight. Mother watched me from across the table as Daisuke placed the small dishes of food before us.

"Hungry?" she asked.

"I've never felt hunger like it," I admitted.

Mother laughed. "I'm glad to see your health has returned. Now, eat."

The meal looked like a feast. One dish carried *Mochi* rice cakes. Other dishes bore spinach, pickled ginger, and *nori* seaweed. I looked up at Daisuke in surprise and he bowed his head in acknowledgment.

"Our warrior monks are excellent cooks," he explained. I picked up my chopsticks. "It's all for you, Kimi," said Daisuke, as he poured me a cup of green tea.

I was surprised. I did not want to appear rude, but how would I eat all of that food on my own? "I'm not sure I can eat all of . . ." A smile appeared on Daisuke's face, and I felt myself smiling back.

"Are you teasing me?" I asked, as Moriyasu giggled.

Daisuke shrugged his shoulders. "Monks don't tease," he said.

"Really?" I asked, but I didn't believe him. "Then, I will just have to eat it all—under your orders." I reached out with my chopsticks for the largest rice cake and popped it into my mouth, chewing hard. I nodded my head at the food. "We'll have to get more," I said, "because this won't be enough for me." We all laughed, including Mother.

Then everyone rushed in with chopsticks, and I

pretended to try and fend off each of them.

"Aren't you eating?" I asked Daisuke, once the laughter had subsided.

He shook his head. "I ate earlier. And besides, my job here is to guide you back to good health." He pushed a dish of deep purple *nori* toward me. I took a mouthful and relished the salty taste of the soya dressing as it hit my tongue.

As I ate my first real meal in days, Moriyasu explained the rules of Go to me.

"It's really simple," he said between mouthfuls. "Black pebbles against white pebbles. I need to conquer you, or you surround me. What could be easier?" He tried unsuccessfully to hide a smile.

"What is it? Why are you smiling like that?" I asked.

"Perhaps it's not quite as easy as your brother suggests," Daisuke said. "There are two aims in the game. To conquer territory and to avoid capture. Spread your stones and you gain territory on the board. Keep your stones close together and you avoid capture. But the dual aims of safety and ambition can be . . . challenging." He looked up at me. "Only the best strategist can win, Kimi. And it takes time and patience to conquer your foe. Samurai use this game to improve their strategic planning as soldiers."

"Interesting," I said, my glance darting toward the

47

smooth wooden board. It sounded like just the kind of game I would want to win at.

"Food first," Mother said gently.

Silence fell around the table as we all carried on eating. I lifted my chopsticks again and again until my belly became tight as a drum. I put my chopsticks down.

"Now may we play?" I asked, and Mother smiled and nodded.

Mother and Moriyasu followed as Daisuke and I went to kneel beside the board. Daisuke gave me a bowl of white pebbles; he took the glossy black ones.

"Take a pebble between your index and middle finger and place it on the board," he said. "Put it on an intersection between squares." I gazed at the empty board. It gave me no clues as to what I should do. I looked up at Daisuke.

"Where?" I asked. "There are so many squares."

"That's the whole point!" Moriyasu burst out excitedly. He gripped my shoulder as he peered at the board. "Your choices decide the game."

I stared at the board. The corners called out to me. They looked safe and protected. I picked up a white pebble as Daisuke had told me to and went to place it on an intersection close to the right-hand corner. I brought it down on the board with a *click*. I looked up at the monk uncertainly. He nodded once.

"A safe choice," he said. Doubt immediately plunged through me.

"Is safe good?" I asked.

"Safe is . . . safe," Daisuke said. I sank back on my heels. I'd had enough of being safe, hiding and waiting in that village hut.

The two of us continued to play, taking turns bringing our pebbles down on the board. I decided to play more bravely, beginning to establish a second territory of white pebbles farther into the board's center. Daisuke naturally took the opportunity to surround me and clustered his black pebbles close to mine. At one point, one of my white pebbles was looking vulnerable; if Daisuke brought one more black pebble to surround my pebble, it would be captured. He brought another black pebble down on the board with a sharp click. My breathing turned shallow as I saw what Daisuke had failed to notice; a small cluster of my white pebbles edged his latest black pebble. When he captured my white pebble, I would be free to capture his black stone. I was making a sacrifice in order to further my game.

"Sorry, Kimi," Daisuke said as he lifted my white pebble off the board and threw it into the small bowl by his side.

I forced a displeased look onto my face. *Hide what you're thinking,* I told myself. *Don't let him see.* But there was no point wasting any more time. I picked a white pebble out of my bowl and held it in the air, pretending to consider. Then I brought it down on the board with one swift movement, and Daisuke gave a small cry of disbelief. At the last moment, he had noticed what I had been watching for an age—his vulnerabilities. I plucked his final black pebble from the board and placed it in my bowl. Then I looked back up at Daisuke.

"No, I'm sorry," I said. "It was too good an opportunity to miss."

From then on, I had the advantage, placing my pebbles down one after the other, capturing his at a rapid rate until it was clear that he had been defeated.

"Yes!" Moriyasu cried, punching the air. Daisuke gave a smile and raised his eyebrows in surprise.

"You've learned quickly," he said. "I'm impressed. That was a clever—and risky—strategy for someone so new to the game."

"Kimi is always brave," Moriyasu told him, leaning over the board.

"I can believe it," Daisuke said. But he wasn't looking at my brother; he was gazing straight at me.

Daisuke got to his feet. Moriyasu scrambled to take his place opposite me.

"I have lessons with my master," he said. He started

to walk out of the room. Then he paused and turned back around to look at me. "But this short game shows that you have *ki*, fighting spirit, Kimi. Just like the samurai warriors who play Go." As I watched him turn into the walkway, I felt a rush of pride.

Mother came to kneel on one side of the low table as Moriyasu shook the pebbles back into their bowls, ready for a new game. All this talk of strategy had brought back my thoughts of our fight against Uncle.

"What are we going to do next?" I asked Mother.

Her face remained expressionless, even though I was sure she knew I was asking about the family and Moriyasu's claim to Father's title. Moriyasu was bent over the board, considering his first move.

"We wait," Mother said, after a long silence.

"What for?" I burst out. "Uncle grows more powerful by the day!" Too late, I realized my impertinence. "Forgive me," I said as I bowed. It was difficult adjusting from making decisions to being just a daughter again. Mother allowed the moment to pass before speaking again.

"For one thing, we must wait for your sister to return to full health. But, more important, I've been talking to the monks. The power struggles between the estates and the clans are growing. They're pulling and pushing between themselves. I don't want your brother to get cast to one side while there is such political chaos. His rightful claim to your father's title cannot be lost in the tussle."

As she spoke, the clicking sound of a pebble landing on the Go board drew my attention back to my game with my brother. Moriyasu's first pebble sat in the middle of the board, alone and vulnerable. He looked up into my face hopefully. "Your turn," he challenged.

How could I know what he was planning? From his place in the center of the board, he would be able to group a territory in almost any direction. If I tried to surround him, he could just as easily surround me. Was he drawing me out—encouraging me to take similarly dangerous risks? I realized I had so much to learn.

I looked back at my mother. "You're right," I said reluctantly. "We are only a few small pebbles on a vast playing board. We must make our moves carefully."

CHAPTER SIX

With food in my stomach, I slept well that night. But dawn light soon crept under my eyelashes and teased me awake. The scratches on my back did not hurt as much as they had yesterday.

There was shallow breathing close by. Moriyasu had come to my bed in the night and now he lay by my side, curled up like a mouse. I smoothed a lock of hair away from his forehead. He squirmed in his sleep and snuggled deeper into the warm bedcovers. I gazed past him and saw our mother sleeping in her own bed. Her cheeks were as smooth as marble, but a frown furrowed her brow.

From the open window sounds drifted up from the courtyard, even at this early hour. Curiosity found me pushing the bed covers to one side. Carefully I stepped around Moriyasu. But as I wrapped my quilted robe around me, I froze. My headdress had come off in the night. The midnight-blue silk lay across the dove-white pillow.

The betrayal of sleep had washed over me. I had almost forgotten. In my dreams I still had my glossy hair. I touched the cracked skin on my head to find stubble beginning to graze the surface unevenly. I should have been happy that I was healing, but a sob caught in my chest when I realized how I must look. *What kind of a girl has stubble on her head?* I took a deep breath and leaned over to retrieve the silk, carefully wrapping the square back around my head. With a few clumsy tucks and awkward knots, the ugly truth was hidden once more.

I walked to the slightly open screen and breathed in the cool morning air. A breeze brushed against my cheeks, and I closed my eyes as I listened to my heartbeat slow.

A cry carried up on the air and I pushed the screen open farther to gaze into the courtyard. The warrior monks were training. I could see a group of them holding long, wooden *bokken*. Other monks kneeled, well poised and watching. Their faces were portraits of perfect serenity, reminding me of my sister. They wore loose linen clothes, their sleeves tied back with *tasuki* cords. The legs of their *hakama* trousers were hitched up through their belts in order to allow them to move more freely. None of them wore armor. I knew that even the edgeless swords could deliver painful blows and broken ribs. Every movement counted. As I watched their strikes and parries, I felt excitement course through my veins. I longed to be down there with them, practicing my own sword movements.

I looked back at Mother, on her thin mattress. My heart told me that she would prefer me to stay close by, but I needed to escape. I had spent too many days hiding indoors. Tiptoeing past her, I told myself it would be better for both her and Moriyasu if I left them to their sleep. I did not want to wake them as I paced the room like a caged animal.

The moment I stepped onto the walkway, I looked down to the room where Hana lay. I had not seen her since yesterday and wanted to go to her first. I pushed open the door and saw her laid out on the bed.

She had not moved.

No one else was in the room, though clouds of incense still filled the air. I stepped across the cool wooden floor and kneeled beside her bed. In the weak morning light I thought I could see a smile playing at the edges of her mouth.

"Hana?" I took up one of her hands and held it to my chest, but her fingers drooped uselessly against my palm. I squeezed her hand once, hoping to feel her fingers affectionately squeeze back, but her hand remained cold and lifeless in my grip.

I saw a cup of green tea resting on the table beside her bed. When I felt the sides of the cup, it was cold. Still, I dipped a finger in the tea and brought a few drops to my sister's lips. I brushed my finger against her mouth, hoping that she might respond.

Nothing.

I sighed and gazed down at the folds of bedcovers that covered the worst of my sister's injuries. I did not dare look again; it felt disrespectful to pull the bed-covers back if I was not tending to her.

"I'm here. Waiting for you," I told her. I had no idea if she could hear me. I had no idea if she would ever be able to hear me again. But I remembered a poem from our nursery days and decided to share it with my sister as she lay silently in her bed. I recited

Furious mountain winds in their passing
must spare this spot
For red maple leaves are clinging
even yet to the branch.

I stood up. I hoped that Hana still clung to life, as the maple leaves clung to the tree. I waited, one last moment, for a sign. Then I turned and walked out of the room.

Gravel crunched under my feet as I stepped into the courtyard. One or two of the younger warrior monks looked up at the sound, but soon turned back to their practice. Cautiously I stepped around the edge of the yard toward where an older monk sat, fingering his prayer beads. I took a step back into the shadow of the walkway, feeling suddenly shy.

"Come," said the monk, patting the ground next to him. "Kneel." I hesitated. Why would this monk want to talk to me? But I sat by his side. He did not look at me, but kept his face straight ahead as the warrior monks practiced.

"I sense your philosophy is the same as ours," he said at last. "You live in the heart more than the skin. That is good." Involuntarily my hand flew to my head. But as the monk turned his face toward me, I saw a milky white film over his eyes. He was blind. But if he couldn't see . . . how did he know so much about me?

"I could tell by your footfall that you are a girl," he said as if he could hear my thoughts. "I have heard all about the two girls and their bravery. Will you join our friends in their practice?" As he spoke, he lifted a sword from the ground beside him and held it out to me, hilt first.

For a blind man to handle such a weapon so confidently, knowing where the hilt was and how to avoid the deadly blade—it took my breath away. I found my fingers wrapping around the hilt. The weight of the sword felt good in my hands.

"Go," the monk said, turning his face back to the practice area. "Show me what you can do."

"But how can you . . . ?" I didn't know how to continue. How could he see my sword practice? How could he assess what I was doing? The monk smiled and waved a hand before his eyes.

"The body is our outer shell—and not a good one at that. It lets us down, as I know all too well. I don't need eyes when I can hear the thud of your foot or the sound of the blade. And I can sense your spirit. What more do I need to enjoy the pleasure of your performance?"

I gazed up at the piercing blue sky and my vision blurred as I felt tears sting my eyes. Here I had been, wallowing in my injuries when . . . how could they compare with the losses of this sightless monk? But his words about my spirit had touched me most of all. I had always had the spirit to fight, and after the attack on the village, that spirit had only grown.

I found myself walking over the gravel, holding the sword in front of me. The skin on my back stretched oddly, but it only hurt a little. I wanted to practice, wanted to feel a sword in my hand out in the sunshine.

The sounds of exertion were all around me as the monks swiveled their swords against imaginary enemies. Did they hate the people they attacked in their practice, just as I hated Uncle? I watched the monks as they moved through the well-rehearsed pattern of their *kata* sequence. I noticed that they left a pause between moves that was slightly longer than the pauses we had been taught by Master Goku. With each resting moment, they stared intently at the space before them. I decided to mimic their pattern, to see if there was anything I could learn. I circled the sword until I grasped it above my head. I sliced through the air—and paused. Then I brought the sword into the next position, and waited again. But my stance was not steady and I stumbled slightly to one side as I tried to keep my gaze fixed before me. The blind monk might not have been able to see my performance, but I knew he would be able to hear the scuffs in the gravel as I fell out of line.

I had thought the longer pauses would make the practice easier. Now I could see that they gave me too much time to think. With each slow move from one position to the next, errant thoughts wormed their way into my mind. *Will Hana ever wake from her sleep? What would it take to stop Uncle—if he even could be stopped?* And with each thought, a new emotion pulsed through me. I stumbled again and angrily brought myself back into position. Sweat sprung out on my palms and the sword shifted in my hands.

The only sound I could hear was the thud of my

own heart. I gave up on following the monks' meditative practice, on giving myself time to rest. *This is for you, Uncle,* I thought. I heaved the blade of the sword down to slice through the air. But as I brought it around to my left, I felt the clash of wood on wood.

I swirled around.

My *bokken* had been parried by another sword.

CHAPTER SEVEN

T he blind monk slowly circled around until he stood before me. His face was as serene as ever, but I could see his knuckles were white as he brought his own sword up to chin level.

"You are skilled, Kimi," he said. "But anger drowns your skill. Your emotions turn your sword into a weapon against yourself." He indicated that someone was standing behind me, and I turned to see that Daisuke had been watching. He stepped into the courtyard and accepted the *bokken* that the blind monk passed to him.

"Face each other," the monk ordered, groping to find our shoulders and straighten us up face-to-face.

"Daisuke, you must help show this girl how to adapt to our practice. I would fight her myself, but . . ." A low chortle escaped him and Daisuke grinned at me. I forced a smile back; the anger had still not left me and it was difficult to be as lighthearted as these men. Especially when I felt like such a failure.

"Don't blame yourself," the monk said. *Can he see*

into my thoughts? I wondered. "We make each tiny part of each movement count much more. This means there is more beauty to it—and more to get wrong. Your core must be strong, your movements fluid, and your mind empty. Is your mind empty?"

"No," I admitted.

"Then clear it!" he ordered. Even Master Goku had never been this abrupt with his students. But it was difficult to take insult at this wise monk's teaching; I wanted to learn.

The monk stared into the space between Daisuke and me, but I knew his senses were trained on both of us.

"Are you ready?" he asked, his voice firm.

"Yes, Kazuo," said Daisuke, bowing his head. I did the same.

The monk nodded, satisfied. "Now, Daisuke. Attack!"

Before I had a chance to think, Daisuke drove his sword toward me. I had to hurry to bring up my own sword. I gasped loudly as I twisted awkwardly at the waist. All wrong! Daisuke raised his sword over his head and then brought the full weight of it down on my *bokken*. I slid my blade down the length of his sword and twisted to deflect him to one side. But Daisuke's sword quickly sliced back up through the air and crashed into mine. My *bokken* clattered onto the gravel at my feet and I rubbed my wrists.

Daisuke gave no apology.

"Pick it up," Kazuo said. With my cheeks flushing, I retrieved my sword.

"Who is it you hate so much?" asked Daisuke.

I straightened up and held my sword high and proud before me. My eyes narrowed. "My uncle . . . ," I hissed.

"Your father's killer . . . ," he said.

Pictures of my father and older brothers lying in pools of their blood filled my head. I felt my face harden as anger swept through me. My jaws clenched until they hurt and my hands trembled as I struggled to keep my sword raised.

Daisuke leaped forward, his feet as light as air, and suddenly the tip of his sword hovered beneath my chin. He had taken advantage of my emotions to win the fight.

"You are too good for me," I said.

Kazuo shook his head. "Not too good for you," he said. "Only better than you—now. But keep practicing, remember what I said. Don't forget your spirit." Then he walked away, holding out a hand to feel the outer walls of the monastery.

"He is right," Daisuke said. "While anger remains in your heart, your spirit will never win the fight that counts."

Daisuke brought his sword down and let it hang by his side. His words echoed in my mind but I could not let go of the anger.

"Come with me," Daisuke said, and the two of us walked away from the training ground. Daisuke led me toward a large building that squatted low in the complex. Thick wooden pillars lined the front of the building, and the shutters at the windows were all drawn closed.

"Where are we going?" I asked.

"I'd like you to see something," Daisuke said as he held open the door. "My patients."

I stepped into the gloom. A tall man moved forward to greet us. His head was closely shaved and fine lines fanned away from the corners of his eyes. He held a wooden bowl of water and I could see that his finger joints were knotted with age. But he stood tall and straight.

"May I introduce my teacher, Master Satoshi," Daisuke said. "He is also the head monk at our monastery." I lowered my head respectfully. When I looked back up, I saw the older man dart a questioning look at Daisuke.

"I am showing Kimi the infirmary," Daisuke explained. "I thought she might be able to help."

"Very good," the master said. "An extra pair of hands is always welcome." Then he stepped back.

Groups of people sat around, talking quietly among themselves. Elsewhere, rows of bodies slept or rested on mats. As I took a step closer, I caught my breath. One of the nearest men sat with his back to me. Each nub of his spine poked through his sallow skin. The curved rows of his ribs pushed against the flesh.

The man gazed over his shoulder at me and the dark circles under his eyes spoke of more than sadness. They traced the path of starvation. His body was covered in bruises where he had no flesh to protect him from even the slightest knock, and as he raised a bony hand and smiled at me, I could see where his gums had shrunk back far from his teeth. Forcing myself to remain composed, I raised a hand in salute to him.

"Welcome," he said, before turning back to his friends. I could barely believe that a man so close to death was ready to smile and welcome me.

Daisuke walked past me toward the man, and I followed. The master had turned away to tend to a woman who sat in a corner of the room, murmuring to herself.

"Good morning, Akira," Daisuke said, kneeling next to the man. "Is your health returning?"

The man shrugged his skeletal shoulders. "With your food and medicine, yes," he said. Then his eyes turned serious. "My wife fares less well," he admitted.

"She cannot bring herself to eat."

Daisuke looked around at me and nodded in the direction of a woman laid out on a mat. "See to her," he said gently. "Offer comfort."

I stumbled forward, hardly knowing what to do. Despite all the killing I had witnessed, I had never seen anything like this. I felt ashamed of my good health. Why had I been so concerned about a few scars, when these people's hearts were fluttering weakly in their chests, barely keeping them alive?

I kneeled at the woman's side.

"May I help you?" I asked, my hands knotting in my lap. The woman slowly opened her eyes and looked at me. Then she smiled a weak smile, before shaking her head. Daisuke came to stand next to me and handed me a small bowl of steaming, watery soup. I took it gratefully—it gave me something to do. I placed the bowl on the floor and put an arm around the woman's shoulders. The feel of her bones against my plump arm sent a shudder through me. I lifted her so that she was sitting up—it was like batting a hand through a wisp of fog, she was so light. I raised a spoonful of soup to her dry, cracked lips but she twisted her head away violently.

"I cannot," she said. "My stomach is too shriveled to take anything." I couldn't believe it. The starved were starving themselves now.

"You must," I said, wishing I could say or do more to stir the woman's spirit. But what could I do? And then it came to me. I reached up and slipped the silk scarf from around my head. The woman's eyes widened as she took in my scars and burns, the patchy growths of hair and the tender skin. Under her gaze, the soreness of the area returned to me—as if the scars and burns had been woken up.

"Are you one of the daughters of Yamamoto?" asked the woman. "The ones who were caught in the fire? The girls we've heard so much about?"

I nodded. "And one thing I have learned is that you can never give up."

The woman looked at me, understanding. Then she gripped her fingers around my hand and tentatively brought the spoon to her lips, taking a few small sips as her hand trembled. She closed her eyes as she swallowed and grimaced at the discomfort. But it was a start. I sat with her until the bowl was gone and then climbed to my feet.

Daisuke was a short distance away, watching. I walked over to him.

"Where are all these people from?" I asked as I followed him on his circuit of the room. He was giving people ground herbal powders to add to their bowls of soup.

"The countryside," he said. "They had nothing left

67

once their meager supplies were taken for the *Jito*." I saw a flicker of anger in his face as he bent to a child resting in her mother's arms. "I do what I can."

"Kimi!" a voice called out excitedly, and I was surprised to see my brother sitting with two other children in a corner of the hall.

"What are you doing here?" I asked. Moriyasu didn't seem at all affected by the illness that surrounded us.

"These are my friends," he said. A boy and a girl grinned up at me. Their bellies were swollen but their teeth were white and healthy and I could see the empty soup bowls by their side.

The girl lifted a straw doll up to me. "This is you," she said. "Moriyasu told us all about how you defeated the evil *Jito*'s son."

"The wretched Ken-ichi!" her brother added. His eyes crinkled in a smile as he looked up at me. "He was really awful. But you took care of him. You swung down from a tree and knocked him out with your feet and then you fought him until your blade ran with blood and he was begging for mercy. Isn't that right, Kimi?"

I couldn't help laughing. My brother had clearly been embroidering the details—there had been no blood.

But as I laughed I noticed an older boy shift on his

haunches and shake his head. His clothes were clean and well-darned, unlike the rags most other people here were wearing. He had his back to us, so I could not see his face—but I could feel his disapproval. *Perhaps I should not be laughing here,* I thought.

"What have you been telling them, Moriyasu?" I said.

"About how brave you've been," he said somberly. I did not have the heart to reprimand him for his tall tales. He turned back to his new friends. "And did I tell you about when she was caught in the burning hut?"

The girl turned to me and put a hand up to gently stroke the charred skin of my head. "Poor thing," she said. I could barely believe that a starving child felt sorry for me.

"I'm fine," I said, scrambling to my feet. I was uncomfortable with her sympathy. "I hope you are back to full health very soon, too."

"We will be!" the children chorused.

Moriyasu nodded seriously. "I've told them that if they pray every night to the Buddha, he will make them as strong and brave as you, Kimi."

The girl and her brother nodded eagerly. I smiled and turned away. I didn't want them to see the tears that were brimming in my eyes.

Daisuke was talking with his master, and I

overheard the elderly teacher ask for help with the laundry. I caught Daisuke's eye and he beckoned me to follow. We walked out into a small courtyard, where a wooden basin sat, full of hot, soapy water. Clouds of steam melted away into the morning air.

"I have to wash these blankets," he said. "The fleas need to be kept under control."

"I can help," I said, bending down to pick up the first blanket. "I've dealt with worse than fleas in my time," I said. Daisuke laughed and came to kneel on the other side of the basin. I plunged my arms into the scalding water and rubbed the blanket together between my fists. I knew from my duties at the dojo that the rubbing had to be vigorous.

"I'm impressed," Daisuke said. Splashes of soapy water blossomed on his loose monk's robes.

"Don't be," I said. "Until my uncle killed my father I didn't know how to clean. But I learn fast." Daisuke bent his shaved head to the task.

"What's inside," I began, still washing the blankets. "It's because of Uncle Hidehira, isn't it?"

Daisuke nodded. "It is," he agreed, taking out one of the blankets and wringing it out. "But don't be fooled, Kimi. These people do not waste their spirit feeling angry—their ability to endure is what's keeping them alive. They have found some of the peace you must seek, in order to heal."

I heard Daisuke's words, but I failed to understand. "Why aren't they angry? Why don't they rebel?" The thought I couldn't say out loud came again to me: Were Hana and I the only people prepared to actually take the fight to Uncle? I could feel my hands curling into fists around the wet sheets.

Daisuke straightened up and looked pointedly at my clenched fingers. I forced my hands to relax. "In this monastery, there is much you can learn," he said. "Those people in there taught me a lot."

"What do you mean?" I asked.

Daisuke's eyes clouded with sadness. "I arrived here when my mother died," he said. "She was the only family I had. My sadness consumed me, and the monastery took me in. But it was only when I became involved in helping the ill and the starving of our country that I learned to live again. I let go of the bitterness about my mother and let these suffering people help me find my path in life, to help others with the medicine I'm learning. You could learn from them, too. You could find your own path in life."

A voice sounded out from the sick room. It was Daisuke's master, calling for him.

"I must go," he said with a bow as he turned to the open door.

I knew my path, to face down Uncle, but could it be that my anger was holding me back? Did I need to heal, like those sick people?

Something in his words rang true, deep inside.

If helping the infirm helped Daisuke find his path, then I would do it, too—starting with my sister.

That evening my sister's bandages needed changing. As the stars twinkled in the sky above, I made my way along the galleried walkway. There was no voice to greet me as I let myself into Hana's bedchamber. She remained as still and serene as a painting.

When Daisuke arrived to supervise, I peeled the bandages away from her skin, being careful not to hurt her. A faint sweet aroma rose up from the dirty bandages as they fell in a pile at my feet.

"We will change her bandages every day," Daisuke said. "Her wounds must be allowed to breathe in order to heal. Otherwise there is the danger of infection."

Daisuke gently applied cattail pollen to the wounded area. Then I picked up fresh rolls of linen and wrapped them around her charred limb. Daisuke watched me for a moment, then wandered over to peer through the open screen.

"What is it?" I asked, gently pulling the bedsheets back over my sister. I bent and kissed her forehead, before joining Daisuke. I gazed out to see what he was looking at, but could see nothing other than the inky blue of the night sky. It looked serene. So why did Daisuke seem so unhappy?

"The air. It's . . ." His voice faded away. I took a deep breath, but all I could smell was the incense of the sick room. Daisuke shook his head. "I don't mean that," he murmured. "It's something else." I could see a vein pulse in his temple. Then suddenly he turned from the window and rushed across the room. "Something's wrong; I don't like it. I'm going to find out what it is," he said. There was a tone in his voice that I had never heard before—alarm.

I grabbed his elbow, turning him around to look at me.

"If there's danger out there, I will go with you," I said. "I *must* protect my family."

"No," Daisuke said, gently pulling away. "It could be dangerous."

"Please," I said. "I have fought before. A good fighter needs a friend by his side. Let me come with you—if only for your own sake."

Daisuke allowed himself a grim smile. "Come on, then," he said, stepping out into the walkway.

He glanced once at me. Then we both broke into a run.

CHAPTER EIGHT

The gravel crunched beneath our feet as we cautiously stepped outside. Above us stood the pagoda, its eaves rising high into the night sky until the curved sides could no longer be seen. The stars twinkled as a cool breeze snaked around my ankles. I shivered. Instinctively I reached a hand to the hilt of my sword, but my fingers closed around empty air. In my haste I had left my sword behind! I looked at Daisuke and saw that he was without weapons, too. So be it. We would have to rely on our wits alone.

Daisuke stood with his head cocked to one side, his eyes searching the monastery grounds. I strained my ears. For an age—nothing. Then came the tiny, dry sound of a twig snapping outside the monastery wall.

"Uncle's men," I whispered. In my mind, it had to be. Who else would attack a monastery full of warrior monks?

Daisuke shook his head. "Even Hidehira would not dare to bring hostility to our door." I wasn't so sure. I had faced Uncle before and knew what he was capable of. My heart pounded.

I stepped back behind a maple tree; its drooping, red leaves provided perfect cover. Daisuke understood my thoughts and followed me. Then he pointed toward the monastery walls. I narrowed my eyes and watched carefully.

The shadows of the night began to change and shift. From between the leaves of the maple tree I saw three ebony columns separate, their shapes moving fluidly. The silver light of the moon caught on the folds of the black outfits as the men moved noiselessly.

Ninja!

They were known as the "knives in the dark," the "black-clad assassins." They swore allegiance to no master. They had only benefactors—wealthy cowards who sought dishonorable ends to their disputes. Ninja could slip through the night and stop the heart of any foe. And now they were here, scaling the monastery walls.

One by one, they softly dropped down to the ground inside the monastery. I could see that they were each wearing a black shirt tucked into a sash and their heads were wrapped in black cowls that kept their faces hidden. Silently they returned hooked ropes to their sashes.

Air hissed between my teeth as I drew a shocked breath. Daisuke's eyes had narrowed to slits as he watched their movements. We waited to see what the ninja would do next. Until we understood their plans, we could not contemplate a counterattack.

The ninja moved from building to building. Their feet did not disturb the gravel and I marveled at how three men could move so lightly on their feet.

One of them paused by the side of a building and brought out a tapered cylinder. He kneeled on the ground and held one end of the tube against the wooden wall. Then he placed his ear against the other end. I knew what this was—a listening device! The ninja was trying to spy on conversations inside the monastery. I shook my head in disgust. Where was the honor in such activity? But at least now we knew what the ninja were doing.

They were looking for someone.

Daisuke and I shared a long glance and I nodded. It was a signal to move.

Slowly the two of us crept out from our hiding place. We had to pick our way carefully to avoid the *tetsubishi* that the ninja had scattered behind them. I knew that these were nothing more than the dried seedpods of water chestnuts, but with their sharp spikes they could be painful underfoot and warn the ninja of our approach.

We drew closer and I could feel energy pulse through my veins. One of the ninja had disappeared—moving without our noticing. There was no turning back now. We had to continue our approach toward the two ninja that remained, still listening at the walls of the monastery.

Every sense was strung tight and even the sound of my own breathing seemed to crash in my ears. I tried to imagine that I was as sleek as a cat, creeping up on a mouse. Now I was close, close enough to . . . I raised a hand into the air, ready to give a blow to the back of a ninja's neck.

But someone caught my hand and twisted it behind my back. Pain coursed through my wrist and shoulder and I collapsed to my knees, twisting around to look up into the face of my foe. I saw the glint of a ninja's eye.

"We knew you were watching from behind the maple tree," he hissed. "Then like lumbering moon bears you crashed toward us." He dragged me to my feet. I barely had time to raise my arms to shield myself before he lashed out with a single, well-aimed punch. As I staggered backward, he grabbed my left shoulder and deftly swung himself up so that his legs straddled my shoulders. He held himself aloft from the branches of one of the maple trees as his legs gripped my neck and squeezed tighter and tighter. I couldn't breathe and my hands grasped uselessly at his thighs.

Desperately I twisted my head and sunk my teeth into the flesh of his calf. He cried out in pain and his legs relaxed their grip, but then I felt myself being pulled backward and falling to the ground as he lightly arched his body and cartwheeled away from me.

"Coward!" I called after him. But I knew that no ninja's heart could be bruised by such an insult.

A cry made me scramble back to my feet—just in time to watch Daisuke deliver a swift kick to the face of another ninja. I spotted the third ninja creeping up on my friend, bringing both hands up on either side of Daisuke's head.

"No!" I cried out, and Daisuke swiveled around just in time to avoid the evil touch of the ninja. Instead, he sent out a punch to Daisuke's chest, but Daisuke blocked him with his left arm and immediately countered with a chopping blow to the ninja's head.

Daisuke was fighting two of the ninja. That meant the third . . .

A fierce kick landed in the small of my back and threw me to the ground. I felt the pressure of the ninja's thumb digging into my kidney as I sprawled uselessly in the dirt. Needles of pain darted through my body. Doing my best to ignore the agony, I twisted onto my back and pushed a foot into the ninja's stomach, grabbing his arms at the same time to throw him over me. The man landed on the packed earth behind me, his skull cracking against a hard stone. In the dark of the night, I saw the white of his eyes glitter as they rolled back in his head and he collapsed in a heap. But there were still two ninja left.

Daisuke ran over to me and pulled me to my feet, pointing at the monastery wall. Silhouetted against the moon, the two remaining ninja waited for us on top of the wall, having escaped Daisuke.

"Can you still fight?" Daisuke asked me breathlessly.

I didn't answer, but ran ahead of him and leaped into the branches of a tree. I scrambled up high enough until I was able to jump down onto the rough stone of the monastery wall. There was a soft sigh as Daisuke landed on the wall a few hands' breadth behind me.

I didn't look around at him and I couldn't look down. Not because I was scared of the long drop to the ground—because a ninja stood before me. He had scrambled across the top of the wall, moving his hands through the air, practicing the hypnotic art of *kuji-kiri*. I noticed the ink-black mark of a ninja tattoo on the pale skin of his inner wrist.

I had suffered at the bewitching hands of ninja before, when one of them had paralyzed me during the capture of our friend, Tatsuya. Now the ninja held his hands up before my face and traced his fingers through the air, drawing horizontal and then vertical lines with his fingertips. The movements left me dazed and I heard him muttering an incantation. I could feel my mind going blank and I barely registered the touch of Daisuke's hand on my shoulder trying to shake me back to my senses as he frantically called my name.

I concentrated all my thoughts on to one single, urgent purpose: to break free of the hypnotism this ninja was casting over me.

Stay strong, I told myself. *Resist.*

With a massive effort I sprang forward. I sent out an open-fisted blow to the ninja's ribs and he crumpled, bending over sharply. I kicked out with my right leg, and the ninja fell into the bushes on the outside of the monastery wall. I peered down, but I could not see him—with a wave of fury, I realized that his black robes blended seamlessly into the night.

Suddenly golden light illuminated the monastery gardens. Warrior monks flooded out of the monastery into the night. I heard Daisuke give a whoop of exultation behind me, and when I looked around I could see that the ninja he had been fighting was hanging from the wall. The only thing that stopped him plummeting to the ground was Daisuke, who grasped the dangling ninja's wrist. A single drop of sweat hung from Daisuke's chin and then fell onto the ninja. As the warrior monks ran over, their *naginata* staffs held high above their heads, Daisuke released his grip and the ninja fell to the ground. The ninja landed lightly, but the monks were waiting for him.

I watched from my vantage point on the wall as the warrior monks went to fight. The ninja I had thrown onto the rock had recovered and rushed to his friend's side. Two left to defeat.

The ninja dodged the swinging *naginata*, but one quick monk brought his staff up above his shoulder and then rammed the butt into the face of one of the ninja. Blood spurted from the ninja's nose and he screamed in pain.

The wounded ninja turned on his heel and leaped to scramble up the monastery wall with the help of his hooked rope. *Not so brave now,* I thought. He looked back at the last ninja left in the compound and called: "We came for the boy. Get him!" Then he disappeared into the night.

The last ninja looked around frantically and tried to roll away from the monks, but one brought his staff around in a smooth arc and crashed it into the ninja's ribs. The ninja collapsed onto the ground. The monk's prayer beads swung from around his neck, catching the light of the moon, as he leaned down and dragged the ninja to his feet, pushing him toward the monastery wall. "Leave this place!" The ninja shook off the monk's grip and climbed the wall after his friend.

"No!" I cried out. I could not believe that the monks were allowing them to escape, not after what we had heard—they had come to find a boy. . . . They had come for my brother, Moriyasu. "They can't get away!" I shouted, turning around on the wall to face the land outside the monastery. These men had been after my brother's life—I would not allow them to escape with their lives. I leaped down into the dense vegetation.

"Kimi!" Daisuke called after me.

I ignored him and ran through the long grasses, the dry blades stinging my exposed skin. For the sake of my brother, I could not stop running—even when I felt a low branch tear the head scarf from my scalp. "Get back here, cowards!" I called out into the night.

My lungs hurt with the effort of chasing these invisible men. I emerged from the vegetation onto the brink of a hill. The land once ruled by my father spread out below me in the moonlight: beautiful, dark, and enigmatic. Holding secrets, hiding ninja. They were nowhere to be seen.

A footstep sounded behind me. I didn't look around; I knew the ninja would already be hidden in the forest far below me. A hand reached out to help me and I took hold of it. I could see the long, tapering fingers that had tended to my sister so carefully.

Daisuke.

"Come back, Kimi," he said. I climbed free of the bracken, allowing the monk's fierce grip to steady me. I stood still and gazed up at Daisuke. His eyes were like liquid.

"They were after Moriyasu," I said. "Didn't you hear what that ninja said? How can they be allowed to escape with no consequence?"

"It is not our task to deal out consequence," Daisuke said, turning back to the monastery. "Remember what I said. We all find our true path in time. The ninja have found theirs. It will lead them to everything they deserve. Everyone you care about is safe; that's all that matters."

"This is not the first time I have fought with ninja," I confessed. "They have taken a good friend of mine. Coming out of the river and kidnapping him from our boat."

Daisuke looked surprised. "Kidnapped? I have only heard of ninja killing, not kidnapping—and then to leave you alive? How did you escape?"

I thought about it. "They were only interested in our friend . . . Tatsuya."

Daisuke frowned. "I will see what I can find out about these ninja who keep coming after those close to you."

As we walked back up the hill to the monastery, Daisuke smiled. "My master will reprimand me for jumping the walls of the monastery. I think it is unprecedented."

The monks held open the doors for us, and as we approached, Daisuke held a square of blue silk between his fingers.

"This belongs to you," he said, dropping it into my hand.

"I'd forgotten," I murmured, as I gazed down at the silk. "I almost felt normal again."

"I don't think I've ever met a girl less normal," said Daisuke, his voice warm with teasing. But when I looked up at him, his gaze was earnest.

Together, we walked through the monastery doors. The waiting monks bowed their heads low in respect.

"You have been very brave tonight," one of them commented to me.

"It is time to rest," Daisuke said. "You should go to your room." I turned to the cool walkways of the monastery. All was quiet and undisturbed inside. I hesitated and looked back. "You won't tell Mother about tonight, will you?" I said, pulling a blade of grass from my trousers. "She wouldn't like me chasing after ninja."

Daisuke nodded. "Don't worry, Kimi. Your secret is safe with me. If anyone asks, I'll tell them you're a terrible fighter." I opened my mouth to protest, but then realized I was being teased again.

"Good night, Daisuke," I said.

"Good night, Kimi," he called after me.

CHAPTER NINE

In Hana's room, Mother and Moriyasu were preparing to retire into beds they had set up on the floor beside Hana.

"Did you see all the lights come on in the monastery?" Mother asked me. "What was going on?"

I looked at my innocent little brother and wanted to hold him tight. But I just shook my head. "I don't know. A lot of the monks had been meditating. Perhaps they were retiring to their rooms."

Mother nodded and lay down in bed. Moriyasu ran over to join our mother and she held the cover open for him as he scrambled to warm his limbs against hers.

"You should get some sleep, Kimi," Mother said as she rested her head against the pillow. Her eyes were already closing.

"I will," I whispered. But I had never felt more awake. I went around the room, pinching the flames out from the candles.

As Moriyasu snored softly, I stepped over him and Mother, curled up on the floor. I sat on the edge of Hana's bed and took her hand. Moonlight drew a silver line down Hana's profile. I leaned forward to peer at her face and saw a trickle of moisture on the faded bloom of her cheek. A tear? I reached out a hand and wiped it away.

"Hana," I whispered. "Have you been crying? Are you awake?" But there was nothing. I sat down at the foot of her bed and watched. For long moments, I did not move and my eyes remained fixed on my sister's face. *Is she remembering the fire?* I wondered. *The pain I have caused her?*

"Please come back to us," I whispered. Then I settled back and waited. My eyes burned with tiredness and my body was aching from the fight against the ninja. But I would not fall asleep. Not while there was hope that my sister might open her eyes.

Behind me, a weak light from the open screen illuminated the room. Dawn was breaking. I had kept my watch, and nothing had happened. But I would not give up. A bird sang a solitary daybreak chorus, and as the gentle warbling filled the room, I saw Hana's eyelids twitch.

"Hana!" I called softly. I took one of Hana's hands in mine. I gazed at her face and—yes, again! I could see her eyes moving beneath her eyelids. This had to be a good sign. But what could I do to help? Hana couldn't hear me.

"Perhaps if I meditate," I whispered to myself. I might be able to send my thoughts to her—give her strength.

I held Hana's hand in my lap and closed my eyes. I allowed my body to relax and cleared my mind, breathing deeply. With each exhale, I allowed myself to sink deeper and deeper. Sounds faded away and the darkness behind my eyelids enveloped me. Even the weight of Hana's hand fell away. I was drifting . . . An image filled my mind.

Hana. Her face broke into a smile as she reached out a hand to me. I felt myself run to my sister. But as I approached, her face grew serious and she snatched her hand away. As I reached out to her, I fell and plummeted down into the dark. When the darkness cleared, a battle raged around me. My sister was fighting samurai, and alongside her, Tatsuya and Daisuke fought against the attack of these armored warriors. I watched helplessly as a soldier ran toward Hana, his sword held high above his head. He brought the sword around in a vicious strike, and I cried out as I saw a single red stain blossom across my sister's tunic. Slashed across the belly! Her sword clattered to the ground as she held her hands over the wound, blood dripping out from between her fingers. I tried to call out but I choked on my sister's name.

I watched her fall to the ground. She looked up and her eyes pierced my soul. She held out a hand to me for a second time as she tried to control the shudders of pain wracking her body. I went to my sister. But as I reached out, her eyes filled with hatred, accusing me of I knew not what.

Then my sister was gone.

Anguish forced my eyes open. The meditation hadn't worked. I looked down into my lap, but something was different. Her fingers were intertwined with mine. Was my sister returning to me?

"Please come back, Hana," I said. "There is so much for you here."

A single red maple leaf drifted in through the open screen. It floated above Hana, dancing in the currents of cool air. It dipped, and its golden edges brushed against her face; then it came to settle on the bed, just above her heart. The red of the maple leaf against the white of her linen bedcover was beautiful. I wished my sister could see it.

I looked up just in time to see Hana's eyelashes flutter and then I saw two glistening crescents appear as she slowly opened her eyes.

"You're awake," I breathed, suddenly aware of the wet tears that stained my face. Hana smiled weakly and looked down at the maple leaf.

"I haven't seen one of these in so long," she said simply.

I burst into tears. I could not hold them in any longer.

"You're back," I sobbed. "You're well again!" Hana reached out to me and this time her hand was solid in my grasp. I wiped the tears away from my face and called out to my mother and brother.

"Hana's awake! Hana's awake!" As my sister weakly sat up in the bed, Moriyasu woke first.

"Hana!" he cried, his young face beaming with delight. He scrambled to his feet and ran to her. Hana laughed.

"I'm weak," she warned him, as he roughly scrambled onto the bed. "But I could take a drink of water." Moriyasu immediately dashed out of the room and ran down the walkway, calling ahead of him for a pitcher of water. Hana and I smiled as we listened to his joyful cries.

Mother had sat up and was watching the two of us.

"My daughter," she said quietly. For the first time in days, her brow was unlined and I could see silent joy brimming in her eyes. She climbed to her feet and came to the bed. Then she leaned over and kissed Hana's forehead.

"Now I have both my girls back," she said. She brought her hands together in front of her chest in a prayer of thanks and bowed her head. When she looked back up at us, tears tracked two paths down her cheeks.

"Welcome back," she said, her voice faltering. "I must find Daisuke immediately," she said. "Don't move."

Hana smiled weakly as Mother left the room. "I'm not going anywhere."

My sister and I were alone again.

Hana looked at me, her eyes searching my face. Her laughter and smiles had disappeared and she reached a tentative hand up to the scarf that covered my head. Instinctively I pulled away.

"What happened?" she asked, face creasing in a frown. I could not bring myself to meet my sister's gaze. I said nothing. How could I tell her about what had happened to me, when her own injuries were so much worse?

"Tell me what happened," Hana insisted. "I need you to be honest with me, Kimi. Everyone else will try to shield me from the truth." I knew she was right. Now was no time to protect my sister. *I should have done that back in the inn,* I thought.

I reached a hand up and pulled the silk away from my head. Hana let out a gasp as she saw for the first time the scars and burns that covered my scalp.

"I remember . . . ," she whispered. "There was a fire, wasn't there? Oh, Kimi . . ."

"It's not so bad," I reassured her. "Sometimes I even forget the burns are there."

"Really?" Hana asked, gazing into my eyes.

I shook my head. "Never," I admitted. "But I care less and less each day."

Hana looked down at her arm.

"Remove the bandages," my sister ordered. I rarely heard such sternness in her voice.

"But—" I began.

"Quickly," she interrupted. "Before Mother gets back and stops you." I knew my sister was right; there was no point delaying. Whatever Hana dreaded would only grow worse in her imagination the longer she had to wait. She needed to see the truth.

Hana watched intently as I unraveled the bandages, careful not to hurt her. I pulled away the last of the soaked linen and heard my sister gasp with pain as the bandages lifted away from her raw skin. Down the length of her arm was a long burn. Healthy skin puckered at the edges of the wound, and the burns were either angry red or yellow from blisters. I could see the signs of healing—the layers of new, fragile skin—but sensed that this would be small consolation to my sister. This was the first time she'd seen what the fire had done to her. I only hoped that the shock wouldn't send her away from me again.

"I'm so sorry, Hana," I said. I looked back up at my

sister, but she did not meet my gaze. She turned her head to inspect the injuries more closely.

"It's something, isn't it?" she said.

I swallowed hard. "The burns are bad, but a wonderful monk named Daisuke has been looking after you." I turned my head away in shame. "I just wish I had never inflicted this on either of us."

Now Hana did look up at me. "This isn't your doing—"

"But if I'd stayed hidden under the floorboards—" I interrupted.

"The soldiers would have found us anyway." Hana cut me off. "We never could have escaped that attack unscathed. This isn't your evil, Kimi. We both know who is responsible—Uncle."

Relief flooded my heart. I had been so worried that my sister would hate me.

I walked over to stoke the charcoal fire that was burning in a corner of the room. I bit my lip as I tried to decide whether or not to tell Hana about my vision.

"What is it, Kimi? Tell me," she called over from her bed. I turned around and saw how beautiful my sister looked, despite her burns. Surrounded by the white linen bedcovers, the pale skin of her face looked almost luminous. I had to tell her.

"I've seen things," I began, looking at the floor.

"I've dreamed of battles. We were all fighting . . . Tatsuya was there . . . I'm so worried about Tatsuya. It's been so long since we have heard anything of him. Daisuke says that it's unusual for the ninja to kidnap people. Normally they kill immediately. So why did they take him, Hana?"

Hana's face turned pinched. She gazed past me and I could see that I had brought back painful memories. "I don't know," she said. "I wasn't completely separated from the world, when I was asleep. I had dreams, too. With every dream I felt Tatsuya's hand guiding me as we practiced with our swords. And with every dream . . ." She stopped.

"I'm sorry," I said. "I didn't mean to upset you."

"I just want to know if he's all right," she said quietly. A fresh tear streaked her face, and now I understood why I had seen that tear on my sleeping sister's cheek.

She had been dreaming about Tatsuya.

A voice came from the doorway. "Welcome back, Hana," Daisuke said with a smile.

My sister turned her face up to him and beamed. It was so good to see her smile again. I watched as Daisuke persuaded her to get back under the bed covers.

"Your body still needs time to heal," he said. "Kimi, please bring me fresh bandages." He didn't say a word about the exposed burns or the pile of dirty bandages that sat on the floor beside Hana's bed—evidence of our hasty rebellion while Mother had been out of the room.

I passed Daisuke fresh rolls of linen.

"Now, leave," he told me, as he began to bind Hana's arm.

"But . . ." I didn't want to abandon Hana—not now that she was awake again.

"You haven't slept all night. Don't think I don't know. Please, go to your room and rest. You'll be no use to us otherwise." Daisuke's tone of voice was kind, but I knew he was serious. I looked over the top of Daisuke's head at my sister. She smiled her agreement with the monk.

Reluctantly I turned to leave. I paused in the doorway and looked back into the room. Hana was laughing gently at some joke Daisuke had made. The monk kneeled at the side of her bed and was tucking in the last of her bandages. Neither of them needed me right now.

I turned and went to my room. It was my turn to rest.

CHAPTER TEN

Sunlight poured over me and teased me awake. I opened my eyes slowly, enjoying the sensation of the floorboards beneath my limbs. Ever since training with Master Goku, living as a servant, I had craved the feel of a hard floor beneath my sleeping body.

The throaty song of a bird made me turn my head to gaze out of the open window and I saw that Moriyasu's bed was empty. So was Mother's. How long had I slept? I got up, stretching my arms high into the air, and went to the window. The courtyard below was busy with people and the sun was high in the sky.

I strode down the walkway toward Hana's room, but as I pushed open the door I saw that it was empty, too. *Where is everyone?* I thought.

I ran back to my room and quickly climbed into a simple pastel-green kimono that had been laid out for me.

"Hana? Moriyasu?" I called hopefully. Perhaps

they were nearby. But there was no response. I quickly turned to race out of the room when I suddenly remembered—my head scarf. There was the piece of silk, crumpled at the end of my bed. I picked up the midnight-blue square and wrapped it around my head. I did not try to find a surface in which to see my reflection, but as my hands passed over my scalp, tucking in corners of the scarf, I could feel that the brittle, cracked skin was turning smooth and soft to the touch once more. It was a relief to think that the burns might one day disappear for good.

I stepped into the courtyard. Some monks were walking back into the grounds through the main gates. They carried large woven baskets over their shoulders with leafy greens dangling over the edges. They had been out gathering in the forest—we would all eat well tonight.

I allowed them to pass and then ran toward the infirmary, where I had met Akira and his wife. Since my last visit there, I knew that Moriyasu was fond of this place. Perhaps my family would be there? I pushed through the doors. Groups of peasants sat around, talking quietly. Master Satoshi moved among them and he nodded once to me in greeting. Along the walls of the infirmary were rows of skeletal bodies, sleeping or . . . I shuddered and pressed the thought from my mind. My eyes ranged around the room.

"Welcome, Kimi!" called Akira, from a corner. He had a damp cloth in his hands and was gently washing his wife's frail limbs. I raised a hand in salute and walked over. I kneeled by the side of the couple and bowed my head respectfully. But my eyes were soon scanning the room again.

"Have you seen any of my family?" I asked.

Akira nodded toward a low paper screen. "Your sister is very beautiful," he said. "Like you."

"Thank you," I said. I took a second cloth from the bowl and helped him wash his wife with the warm water, rubbing the soapy cloth across her frail back. When we were finished, I climbed to my feet.

As I approached the paper screen I could see the silhouette of my sister's elegant posture. Her burned arm was in a sling, tied neatly in a knot at her neck. Someone had helped her out of bed.

"Hello, Hana," I said quietly.

My sister turned to gaze up at me and I could see the happiness brimming in her eyes.

"You've found us," she said. "We didn't want to disturb you. You were in such a deep sleep." She turned back to the woman she was tending. The woman looked ancient, though I guessed that illness had added to her years. Her face was sallow and scabs littered her lips. Brown spots covered the back of her hands and her skin looked paper-thin. She was starving to death.

Hana brought a spoonful of broth to the woman's lips and nodded. Obediently the woman sipped and gave my sister a hesitant smile. Hana dipped her spoon into the broth a second time. Despite her own recent illness, my sister was using her only free hand to feed another.

I turned away so that Hana could not see my emotion. Sometimes it was too much to see how good Hana could be. Could I ever be as worthy? I counted under my breath, waiting for my feelings to subside. When I turned back, Hana was still bent to her work. She had not noticed that the sling had slipped. I could see that the new, raw skin of her healing burns looked stretched and puckered. Her young flesh was ravaged still. Hana glanced up at me, offering a smile. But the smile faded when she saw the expression on my face. Quickly she adjusted the sling.

"There are always scars at first," she said. "Remember how we used to scrape our knees as children? Now we can barely see the marks." Her smile returned, and so did mine. Her talk of our childhood years reminded me of the games we had played with the *nazuna*. Daisuke knew much about healing herbs. Perhaps he could help Hana—could he give us something to help her scars heal over?

"You're right," I said. "I'm sure your scars will heal well."

I scanned the room to see Daisuke, framed by the

light from an open doorway. The copper in his skin shone against his saffron robes. I walked quickly over to him. Turning toward the door, he indicated with a nod of his head that I should follow.

As we stepped outside into the area where the washtubs were, he waited for me to speak.

"What can I do for my sister?" I asked. "It's my fault she's injured. I want to do something to put it right." Behind him, the maple trees swayed in the morning breeze.

"I can help you," he said. He reached out a hand to indicate the low hills beyond the monastery. "The *himawari* plant is rare, but it is sometimes to be found growing out there. It has seeds whose oil can heal."

"Can we go and find it? Now?" I asked.

Daisuke shook his head. "It's not that simple. As I said, it's rare. And I will need permission from my master to leave the monastery. For now, come and help me with something else."

Daisuke led the way out into the larger courtyard, and we sat beneath a cherry tree. It was cool beneath the tree's shade. Daisuke picked up a wooden bowl filled with dried yellow flower buds.

"These can be brewed and the tea can calm even the most turbulent of souls," he explained. "But first we must sift through the dried flowers to make sure that there are no blades of grass or pieces of grit." He placed the bowl between us and we picked through the dusty flower petals, turning over the soft leaves in our hands and brushing off any dirt. I brought my hand to my face and breathed in deeply the pungent smell of the crushed chamomile.

"What is the *himawari* plant?" I asked. I had never heard of it before.

Daisuke turned his face up to the sun and closed his eyes, smiling to himself. "The *himawari* is like sunshine brought down to earth," he said.

I frowned. "Daisuke, I'm sorry," I began. "But I don't understand what you're talking about."

Daisuke laughed. "You will," he said, getting to his feet and taking the wooden bowl. "In time. Now I must see to my patients. But when Master Satoshi says the time is right, I shall take you to find the flower. It will help your sister."

"Thank you," I said. "This means so much to me." I watched my friend step back into the cool of the infirmary. *I am lucky,* I thought, as the door swung shut behind him. *I have made a good friend.*

Daisuke and I stood at the gates of the monastery. Dawn mist swirled at our ankles and I hugged my silk robes tighter around my body, trying not to shiver. I was grateful for my head scarf, wrapped tightly against the slight chill in the air. The morning sky was streaked with washes of pale blue and the sun had not yet peeked over the horizon.

Moments before, Daisuke had come to my room and gently woken me. We were both careful not to disturb my brother and mother as we tiptoed across the floor on bare feet. Once outside the room, Daisuke had passed me a pair of monk's straw sandals.

"They'll be much better for walking through the mountains," he'd explained. I smiled as understanding dawned. We were going in search of the *himawari*.

Now we were setting off. Two warrior monks opened a small door in the huge gates of the monastery for us. Their white cowls shone in the weak dawn light and they lifted their wide-bladed *naginata* staffs to let us pass. Curiosity shone in their eyes, but neither of them questioned us. Daisuke must make these trips often on behalf of Master Satoshi.

"The answer to your wishes is out there, Kimi. Are you ready?" Daisuke asked as we gazed at the vivid, lush greens of the mountain. I nodded and we stepped forward into the forest that edged the monastery. Twigs and leaves snapped beneath our feet and I scanned the trees nervously, looking for any sign of another ninja attack or for my uncle's men. We both had brought our swords with us; we would not face enemies unarmed for a second time. But slowly I began to relax. The trees soared high into the sky above our heads, and birds swooped through the air as they flitted from their nests in search of food. There were no enemies here.

As we walked, Daisuke pointed out things to me. He strode over to a tree wrapped in vines and tore up some of the vine roots, snapping them open to reveal snow-white flesh.

"This is the *kuzu* root," he explained. "It reduces fever. Look out for it if you're ever injured on your travels." He placed the root into a small hemp bag he carried slung over a shoulder. At the base of another tree he spotted a cluster of triangular green stems, and with a piece of bark he dug up clusters of fat garlic. He pointed to his heart.

"This is good for a long life. It helps your heart, Kimi." He brushed the earth from the bulbs of garlic and added them to his bag of precious supplies.

We walked on, Daisuke taking the lead as the sun climbed higher in the sky. I could hear a low rumble up ahead. "What's that noise?" I asked Daisuke. Since their attempt at capturing my brother, I instantly took any strange sound to herald the ninja.

"You'll see," Daisuke replied. We emerged into a grassy clearing and my breath caught in my throat. Ahead was a pool of emerald water, surrounded by velvety moss. And behind that—a waterfall crashing down from the rocks above. I had heard of such things, of course. In poems and stories our nurse would tell us. But I had never before seen such a huge waterfall with my own eyes.

I stepped past Daisuke and kneeled at the side of the pool, dipping my hand into the icy cold water. The waterfall threw up a cloud of mist that kissed my cheeks and cooled my blood. The rocks not obscured by the tumbling white water glistened in the morning sun. I looked back around at Daisuke.

"Is this where the *himawari* grows?" I asked. I had to raise my voice to make myself heard above the crash of water.

Daisuke shook his head and pointed. "Over there," he said. "We need to walk through the waterfall." The monk had not raised his voice, yet his words still sounded clearly in my ears.

Daisuke took the lead. He clambered up from rock to rock toward the falling water, bending over so that he could use his hands to steady himself. I watched carefully to see how he placed his feet and I copied the way he tested each rock before putting his full weight onto it.

Soon we were close to the sheer rock wall, and the waterfall crashed down almost overhead. Just as I thought we could go no farther without being knocked into the pool below, we stepped into a crevice of air between the sheet of water and the rock face behind it. We could make our way behind the waterfall to the other side.

We were caught in a secret world of our own, and it felt like no harm could come to us here.

"Don't fall over," Daisuke called back as we made our way, careful to avoid the clumps of moss clinging to the stones. "I know how clumsy you can be."

"Me?" I shouted over the noise of the water. "You're the one who needs to—Daisuke!"

My friend slipped, lurching forward with a cry, and I grabbed his wrist, stopping his fall just before his ankle twisted badly beneath him. If his foot had become trapped between rocks here . . . I dreaded to think how I would have gotten him back to safety.

Daisuke righted himself and looked over his shoulder at me.

"Thank you," he gasped. "That's what I get for teasing. Let's cross as quickly as we can. But be careful." He pointed to the other side of the pool and I nodded. We were nearly there.

A moment later, I lost my own footing, stumbling into the waterfall. I cried out, but Daisuke didn't hear me.

"Daisuke! Wait!" I called. But it was useless.

I had fallen into a crevice where the water crashed down around my shoulders. If I wasn't careful, I could slip over the edge and fall into the pool below. I gasped in lungfuls of air and forced myself to stay calm. As my heartbeat slowed, another sensation filled me. It was a feeling that had been a stranger to my heart for so long.

Peace.

I pulled off my head scarf and raised my face up to the water that pounded down on me, driving into my skin. The worry and anxiety of the past weeks were being washed away. The icy water stung my skin as my clothes clung to me. I allowed my tears to mingle with the water that coursed down my body, swept away in a shower of water that cleansed my very soul.

Eventually I stepped back onto the rock path and made my way across to Daisuke. He was waiting patiently on the other side of the pool, watching. He reached out a hand and I gripped it as I climbed up onto the mossy bank. As warmth returned to my skin, I noticed that I still felt Daisuke's fingers gripping my hand. I looked up at him. Not a word passed between us, but Daisuke's eyes seemed to be asking me a question. I allowed my hand to rest in his for a moment more. Then, I gently pulled away and started to wring out my head scarf. Daisuke's face reddened and he looked down at the ground, before darting another glance at my face. Our eyes met and neither of us looked away.

"Happiness is found in the most unexpected places," Daisuke said, finally breaking the silence. "Even in places where monks fall over badly and make fools of themselves." I lifted my face to the sky and laughed.

"Kimi!" Daisuke said, climbing to his feet. He pulled me up after him. "Do you know what I've just seen?"

"What?" I asked. He pulled me over to the side of the pool and the two of us peered into the water, side by side. I could see our dual reflections; our faces glowed with happiness. Then I noticed something else. Daisuke brought a hand up over my head and as I turned my face to one side I saw what he had already noticed.

"My hair is growing back!" I breathed. Where once had been stubble and dead skin, now I could see the unmistakable glint of ebony hair catching the light. I put a hand up to my head and for the first time in so long, I felt soft hair.

There was only one thing that made my smile falter: A vivid streak of white ran from above my right eye to the back of my head.

CHAPTER ELEVEN

W hat's happened?" I asked as I turned my head from one side to the other, taking in the vision reflected back to me from the water. "That hair has turned white, like a moon bear's streak!"

Gently Daisuke pulled my hand away from my head and turned me around so I could not avoid the gaze from his intense eyes. "Your experience has changed you," he said.

I turned back to the pool of water and bent over to inspect my reflection again. My brow furrowed as I thought about what Daisuke had said. I realized that he was right. I did not mind this snow-white badge of honor. *I have gazed in the face of death and did not turn away,* I thought to myself. I looked back up at Daisuke and smiled.

"Let's find that plant," I said.

We strode through the long grasses on this side of the waterfall, pushing them aside until we emerged in a small clearing. The space prickled with heat—it was a sun trap. I wheeled around, taking in this small haven.

"The *himawari*," Daisuke said, pointing to tall flowers with huge heads the color of the sun. In the center of each flower was a fat, velvety heart full of seeds. Bright yellow, tapering petals fanned around each flower like a skirt of gold. I walked over to one of the tallest plants. It towered above me. I wrapped my fingers around the green stem. It was prickly under my touch and the stem was as thick as my upper arm.

I turned to Daisuke, but he was over by another of the plants—one that had suffered storm damage and now lay on the ground. He kneeled down and picked the seeds out of the flower's heart, placing them carefully in a pocket sewn into the inside of his hemp bag. He looked up at me and jerked his head to indicate I should help.

I reached up to my own flower to pry the seeds from its head, one by one. There weren't many seeds left; it was clear that the mountain birds had been here first. But I didn't mind sharing this golden treasure with the rest of nature, as long as there was enough left for my sister.

"The seeds contain goodness from the sunshine that we can squeeze out. We'll make an oil to apply to your sister's burns and it will help her heal," Daisuke explained, his voice low as he bent over his work. I gazed at the seeds that lay scattered in the palm of my hand. It was extraordinary to think that these tiny seeds could help something as ravaged as my sister's skin.

Once we had filled his pouch, Daisuke sat back on his haunches and looked at me. "One day, you may know as much as I do about nature," he said. "And if you're very lucky, you might even be able to cure a sniffle."

I laughed and shoved Daisuke's shoulder so that he fell back in the grass. "And if you're very lucky, perhaps one day you will be as nimble as me." I sprang to my feet and ran through the long grasses, back toward the waterfall. I heard Daisuke chuckling as he gave chase.

As we walked back to the monastery, I felt more alive than I had for a long time. A hawk floated in the sky above us, riding the air currents. I raised a hand to shield my eyes and watched its streaked wings as it flew ahead of us—master of its own destiny.

"Do you wish you were as free?" Daisuke said, matching my stride as he walked alongside me.

I shook my head. "I'd rather have my friends with me."

Daisuke looked down at his feet. "So would I," he said. Then, as the monastery walls reared ahead of us, we both broke into a run.

Back at the monastery, Daisuke led me into a small outer building. The smell of incense hung heavy in the air and there were rows of dark-colored bottles arranged on shelves on the wall. Daisuke and I took off our sandals before stepping inside.

Master Satoshi kneeled on a mat. Small bowls filled with powders and petals were aligned before him.

"You've been a long time," he said, without looking up.

"Sorry, Master," Daisuke replied with a bow. "We had to venture beyond the waterfall to find what we were looking for." His face had gone serious and I knew we had left our joking behind. Master Satoshi frowned and turned sharply back to his work. I could see that he was displeased about something. Had we really been gone too long?

"This is where we make our medicine," Daisuke explained in a whisper. He led me over to a shelf of ceramic bottles. "Where healing begins."

"What can I do to help?" I asked.

Daisuke kneeled on a second mat, behind Master Satoshi's. I came to kneel on the other side. Master Satoshi glanced up and gave me a long, steady stare. I had no idea what he made of me. After a moment, he closed his eyes and brought his hands together in front of his chest, bowing his head to mutter a prayer over the medicines he was preparing.

Between Daisuke and me stood a pestle and mortar. Daisuke took out the seeds we had collected and poured them into the mortar. Then he took up a few grains of rough salt, adding them to the small bowl carved out of granite. He pounded with the pestle.

"The salt helps to break down the seeds," he explained, "and it draws out the goodness." He nodded at the ceramic bottle on the table. "Can you shake out a handful of flower heads and add them to the mix?" he asked.

I pulled the stopper out of the bottle, and immediately a pungent aroma of crushed petals filled my nostrils and made me light-headed. I shook out a handful of the dried white flowers into my open palm. My skin felt as though it were being kissed by butterflies' wings.

"It's white lavender," said Daisuke.

"So gentle you can use it on the youngest, most tender skin," added Master Satoshi, his prayers at an end. The master climbed stiffly to his feet and went over to the shelves.

I reached over to add the petals to the mixture in Daisuke's mortar. I watched as he ground down the seeds into a paste. Then Daisuke reached for another, larger bottle and poured some oil into the

112

pestle. A few more vigorous turns of the pestle and we had a smooth, thick mixture. So simple! And yet, I was aware that Daisuke was sharing secrets with me that few others were privileged to witness.

Daisuke smiled at me as he dragged a bottle over the table toward him.

"Daisuke, I will speak with you," said Master Satoshi. My friend shot me a guilty look and then scrambled to his feet and went to join his master beside the shelves. Their heads bowed close in conversation, and I could not hear what they were saying. All I could see were the two lines that furrowed Daisuke's forehead as he listened to Master Satoshi.

Daisuke walked back to me and I gave him a questioning smile as he sat down. But Daisuke did not meet my glance. His face had turned cold and formal.

"Now we wait," Daisuke said as he poured the ointment into another bottle. "It will need to rest for a quarter moon. Then it will be ready to apply to Hana's skin." He closed his eyes, fingering his prayer beads as he blessed the medicine. I bent my head low in respect.

He stood up suddenly and put the bottle on a shelf with several others. As Daisuke led me to the door, I wanted to say something to thank him.

"Daisuke, I . . ." Words seemed to have flown away

from me like swifts darting through the clouds.

"Thank you for your assistance this morning," the monk said. "I hope your sister recovers swiftly." I looked back up at him and searched his face. He was speaking as if we weren't friends at all.

What had Master Satoshi said to my friend to make him turn so cold and stiff?

"Good-bye, Kimi," he said, opening the door. Sunlight flooded into the room, making my eyes hurt. I bent my head to walk through the low doorway.

"Good-bye, Daisuke," I said. But when I turned back around, the door was shut.

Days passed. Hana gained strength with each passing dawn and my back was almost normal. Her arm was still in a sling, though occasionally she would slip it off and rub the feeling back into her arm. Sometimes she would even go a whole morning before putting it on. I knew she was definitely on the mend the day that she started teasing me again.

"Did you enjoy your trip out with Daisuke?" she asked one morning. "It wasn't too . . . tedious for you?" I looked up from folding my clothes and studied her face. I could just see the twitch of a suppressed smile.

"What do you mean? Why would it be tedious?" I asked.

"So it wasn't?" she asked.

I felt the blood rush to my face. "If you weren't still recovering, I'd pinch you on that tender spot on your arm. Remember how you used to hate it as a child?"

Hana pulled away from me, laughing. "I'm glad of my sling, then," she said, quickly slipping it on. "It saves me from pinching sisters. It's okay, you know, to make friends."

The laughter disappeared from my heart. A distance had grown between Daisuke and me since our afternoon gathering sunflower seeds. "At first I thought we were friends, but now I'm not so sure. Can monks have friends?"

"Of course they can," said Hana. "They want to promote peace and harmony—exactly what friendship is all about. Perhaps it's just his other obligations that are keeping him busy."

It was true. Every day, Daisuke would be in the infirmary tending to the people. And every day, when Hana and I went to help, he would see me and give a polite smile and nod—nothing more.

I focused on the work, and it gave me hope to see that some people were getting stronger with Daisuke's help. But for others the starvation had gone on for too long and there was no way back. I would feel the blood rush through my veins as a cover was pulled up over another set of sunken cheeks. Then I would have to go outside.

My own injuries healed neatly; Hana said that she

could barely see the scrapes on my back anymore.

And every day I practiced with my sword. The warrior monks became used to my joining their ranks, parrying invisible enemies. I learned much surrounded by these men—so powerful, yet so serene. They had cores of steel beneath their saffron robes, and I prayed that one day I would attain the inner strength that they had spent a lifetime honing.

One morning, I walked into our room, fresh from sword practice, to find Mother sitting on a black mat at a low table, her delicate features outlined by the sunshine. Beside her on the table was a small ink stone and a *fude* brush, the tip soaked in black ink. A scroll of *washi* paper lay before her, one end weighed down to stay open, and I could see that she was drawing fluid strokes across its surface.

I came up behind her. My mother's writing was beautiful. Each character followed the strict order of strokes, her brush was never too soaked in ink, and her movements flowed precisely across the paper. All of these things she had striven to pass on to me, but I proved a poor student.

"Good morning, Kimi," Mother said. She didn't look up from what she was doing.

"Who are you writing to?" I asked. We had spent so long hiding from the world that it made me nervous to see my mother writing a letter.

116

"The Shogun," she replied, putting down her brush. She looked up at me. "He is the most powerful man in Japan—he has the power to declare Uncle's title defunct. Your father always had his respect. I am asking for an audience with him, to put forward the case that Moriyasu's is the rightful claim."

I looked over her shoulder so that I could read the paper more easily. I could see no mention of Uncle or his foul actions, about his taking over estates. Instead, I read snatches of "it would be my honor" and "devoted servant." At one point, Mother had even said that she would be happy to kneel at the Shogun's feet! I glanced back up at her, but she had picked up her brush again and was bending over the paper.

"You haven't said anything about what's really happened—" I began.

"Shush, Kimi." Mother cut me off. "This is a delicate matter and the Shogun is a very important person. I must respect the codes of good conduct and tread carefully. There are processes we must go through. There will be time for more . . . frank conversations later. Even then, he might not hear our case. And if he does, there's no guarantee that he'll believe what we have to say. We could be exiled. But because of your father's position we have a hope that the Shogun will see us."

I scrambled to my feet. I wanted to tear the letter into tiny pieces! What was Mother thinking? Exiled? Only a chance he might see us? She stood up beside me and touched the place where the white streak grew in my hair. It was long enough now that it had started to curl around my temples.

"Your white streak is distinguished," she said, smiling. "Just as a girl of your status is distinguished."

I pulled away from her, feeling the anger well up inside me. "But exiled? How will we fight against Uncle if we are banished?"

"Kimi!" Mother said, her brow creasing. She did not raise her voice and she did not have to. I knew when I was being reprimanded. I was letting my anger take control of me, but I could not stop now that I had started.

"I mean no disrespect," I said, struggling to control the trembling in my voice. "But we need action, not words! We have friends in some of the estates. We could go to them tomorrow and I know they would help us fight Uncle." I flung a hand in the direction of home. "All we need to do is say the word."

Mother shook her head sadly. She went back to the table and sealed the letter. "Your friends are not enough," she said. "Uncle has been building his army and is even stronger than before. Only the Shogun's samurai with his allies can stop him." Mother looked up at me and her eyes were brimming with tears.

"You have been so strong, my daughter, but your anger is not enough. This fight is bigger than you or I. We must take it to the Shogun." As Mother ended her speech, her shoulders sagged and she drew her hands up to cover her face. "I admit; I never expected it to come to this."

My anger was not enough. The words echoed in my head and mingled with Daisuke's. Perhaps my anger was preventing me from seeing that my mother was right. Our friends had done much to help us in the past. But now we needed the might of another strong leader—a leader who had the courage to fight for good. Perhaps the action would come from these words. I went to my mother's side and gently took the letter from her.

"I'm sorry I got angry. I'll take the letter to the gate," I said. "The guards will find us a messenger to carry it to the Shogun."

"Thank you, Kimi," she said, the tears drying on her cheeks. "We are doing the right thing, you know." I couldn't know that for sure. But my mother's words had frightened me. *If Uncle Hidehira has become this dangerous*, I thought, *we will need all the help we can get.* The fight would come, but I was going to make sure we had the biggest sword by our side.

The sword of a Shogun.

CHAPTER TWELVE

D ays later, the ointment for Hana's wounds was ready. That morning, Daisuke brought the bottle to me.

"Thank you," I said. "This means so much to us. To me." I waited for a response. Daisuke gave an awkward smile, but when his glance met mine the smile relaxed and his face creased in a grin. I felt relief and hope flood through me. A part of him still wanted to be my friend.

"It's the least I could do," he said. He handed the bottle to me and our fingers touched as I took the cool ceramic from him. "Take care of it," Daisuke said, pulling his hand away. "It is precious."

"I know," I said. There was a pause and so I said, "Thank you for teaching me about my anger. I have not won the battle inside myself, but I have begun to fight it."

Daisuke smiled. "No enemy stands a chance against your determination, Kimi. You will defeat it."

"Daisuke!"

I recognized the sound of that voice by now, calling from outside the infirmary. "Master Satoshi is waiting for you," I said. Daisuke nodded.

"I must go," he said. I waited for him to leave. He hesitated but then turned to stride out into the courtyard.

When he had gone, and my heart had slowed, I carried the bottle into my sister's room.

"I have something for you," I said, light glistening off the narrow neck of the bottle.

"What is it?" Hana asked uncertainly. She stood up from her work mending clothes and came over to take the bottle from me. Her arm was out of its sling now, but her scars were still there beneath the sleeves of her kimonos—angry and red. "It will help your scars heal," I explained. "We are very lucky; Daisuke has shared one of his rare medicines with us."

Hana's eyes searched mine hopefully. "The scars could go away?"

When I nodded, she perched on the edge of her bed and held her burned arm out to me.

"Go ahead, Kimi," she said. "Tend to your patient."

I sat at her feet and rubbed my palms together, warming them. Then I poured some of the precious ointment into my open palm and rubbed the oil between my hands. It felt like liquid gold and the scent of sunshine drifted up toward our faces. I grinned at Hana. I knew this was going to work.

As I rubbed the oil into her skin, I told Hana about the day Daisuke and I had stepped into the clearing to find the *himawari* flowers that worshipped the sun. Hana gasped when she heard how tall they were and I carefully described the large, yellow petals that circled each flower.

"Look, Hana," I said. "See how the skin is glowing now?" As I kneaded and massaged, blood was rushing to the surface of the skin. Hana's lifeblood—to help her heal. I looked up at Hana's face and she smiled.

"It is starting to look better, isn't it?" she said.

"You never stopped being beautiful," I said. I wiped my hands on the cloth and climbed to my feet. "And now you will be even more beautiful. Just don't let it go to your head."

As I turned, Hana threw the cloth at me and it landed over my shoulder. The two of us laughed as I pulled the cloth away and bundled it up into a ball, threatening to throw it back at her.

"Excuse me." A voice sounded from the doorway, and my arm froze in midair. I turned around slowly, and the laughter disappeared from the room when we saw a messenger waiting to speak.

"Mother!" I called. "A messenger is here." As he stepped into the room, Mother arrived. All three of us waited for the man to say something.

He cleared his throat and handed a rolled-up scroll to my mother. She broke the seal and unfurled it. I could see the hand-painted decoration and vertical writing; this was a formal letter. Mother's eyes scanned the words, her knuckles white as she gripped the paper. She opened her mouth to speak, then hesitated, as she noticed my glance flick over to the messenger. She gave me a tiny nod.

"You may leave us now," she said to the messenger, who bowed and backed out of the room. Hana moved after him and shut the screen door.

"It's good news!" Mother said as we crowded around her. Her hands were trembling now. "It's the Shogun's Administrator. He's getting married and wants us to attend. This is it! Our opportunity to seek an audience." Mother walked between us. She sank to her knees and brought her hands up to her chest in a prayer. "I have been so worried," she said. "I didn't know if my letter had found its way to the Shogun— there are so many of Uncle's men out there." She turned back to us. "We must go! Tomorrow, if we are to make it in time for the wedding."

Hana and I watched as Mother moved around the room, sweeping up discarded clothes. I walked over to her and gently took the ivory comb that she was struggling to add to the pile of objects she was already carrying.

Hana joined in with her excitement. My sister ran to the door of the room and flung it open. "Come, Kimi. We have packing to do."

As she strode out into the walkway, she knocked against a person walking past. He was tall and his prayer beads swung against his chest. It was Daisuke.

"I apologize," Hana said, color flooding her cheeks.

Daisuke smiled and turned to look into the room. As I gazed at him, it suddenly struck me that our days together in the monastery were coming to an end. I might not ever see him again.

"I saw the messenger," he said. "Good tidings?" His glance flickered over toward me.

"Oh yes," gushed Hana. "We have been called to the wedding of the Shogun's Administrator. We will be among people of influence. We will be able to—"

"Hana!" Mother interrupted, stepping between my sister and the monk. "You do not need to bore Daisuke with your chatter." Mother bowed to him. "We must go at the break of the day tomorrow. You have been so kind, but now . . . Now we must continue with our journey. Hana is fully healed and Kimi is restless."

Daisuke looked over at me, his eyebrows arched in surprise. I couldn't believe Mother was using me to cover her evasiveness! And why didn't she trust Daisuke with the truth? He had done so much for us; surely he deserved to know we intended to appeal to the Shogun for help in deposing Uncle.

I took a step forward to protest, but as I did so Daisuke brought out a slim key from the folds of his robes. He held it in the air, before passing it to Mother.

"You have been honored guests and have done much to help in the infirmary." He inclined his head toward Hana in particular acknowledgment of her daily visits. "In return, let us do one last thing for you. We have storerooms full of donated kimonos— waiting to be sold in more prosperous times. You will need to present yourselves well in front of the Administrator."

Mother's fingers tightened around the key as she gazed up at Daisuke. "Thank you," she said. "We will, of course, repay you when we can." Then she turned to Hana. "Coming?" she asked. Hana's face lit up and she followed my mother out of the room. Mother turned to me.

"Kimi?" she asked.

"In a moment," I said.

Mother and Hana strode down the walkway,

leaving Daisuke and me alone together. The silence pulsed between us and I wondered who would be first to speak.

"That afternoon after we'd gathered the sunflower seeds," Daisuke began, "when we were in the medicine room with Master Satoshi . . ."

"Yes?" I said. I sensed that my friend was about to come back to me.

"He didn't approve that I'd . . . that I'd become so close to you," Daisuke said. He glanced over my shoulder, out of the window. Clearly he was struggling to find the right words. "He thought I was becoming too attached and that my search for clarity would be disrupted. I am to be the next head monk of this monastery one day."

"Is that why you wouldn't speak to me?" I asked.

Daisuke nodded. "I'm sorry. I've been struggling to do the right thing. A monk's life can be hard, Kimi."

"I understand," I said, wanting to relieve him of the agonized expression on his face. I couldn't help but think, though, that at a few words, Daisuke was happy to give up our friendship.

"Do you?" he asked hopefully, looking back at me.

"We will say our farewells tomorrow," I said, ignoring the question and struggling to keep my voice light. "Let's say them with smiles."

"Yes. Much lies before you," Daisuke replied. "Don't resist your mother. She is working hard to save her family." He threw out a hand, indicating the open doorway. "They are picking out clothes already. Don't you want to choose an outfit?"

It was the last thing I wanted to do. Was Daisuke trying to make up for discarding me by offering pretty dresses? Perhaps he did not know me after all.

I took a deep breath. I didn't want to follow Mother and Hana. It was one thing to go to the Shogun and ask for his help, but why did we need new clothes?

The storeroom was a squat building behind the infirmary, with a single large doorway. I walked inside and waited for my eyes to adjust to the gloom. A lamp swung from the ceiling and gradually I could make out a few boxes piled on rough wooden shelves. Hana was kneeling on the ground, an open crate before her. She pulled out a heavy swath of red silk and held it up against her pale neck. "Look, Kimi!" she said, beaming. "Can you imagine wearing this?"

I couldn't. I had spent too many days and nights in the clothes of boys and paupers. My sister plunged her hands into the box and brought out another kimono. I took a hesitant step forward and felt the embroidered silk. It was icy cold against my touch

127

and I shuddered, pulling my hand away.

"What's wrong?" Hana asked.

I shook my head, not wanting to spoil their happiness. Hana wanted me to try a gold *saishi* head ornament but I stepped back. I could never wear such a thing—not now. Hana put the ornament back in the box, but then Mother stepped out from behind one of the shelves and held out a long, emerald outer-garment toward me.

"Please, Kimi," she said. "Please try." Reluctantly I took the dress from her. Hana cried out in delight as she came across a heavy sky-blue kimono. She pulled it on over her undergarment. Mother came behind her to make sure that the back seam was centered. Then I watched as Hana wrapped first the right side over her body and overlapped it with the left side. Mother brought the sash around her waist to take up any excess of material so that the kimono hung at the right length at Hana's ankles. My sister watched, delighted. It was good to see her so full of life, but something in my heart shriveled at the sight of so much pleasure taken in bolts of silk. *Is this what we've been fighting for?* I thought. *So that Hana could play dress-up? Has she forgotten everything?*

Hana turned to look at me, her face glowing. "You now," she said. Mechanically I brought the kimono around my shoulders. The silk hung in heavy folds, dragging me down.

"Come, come, Kimi," Mother remonstrated. "We have much to do." I brought the sides of the kimono around my body—first the right, then the left— standing as still as a statue while Mother adjusted the belt. "Beautiful," she murmured, almost to herself.

I turned to the open door of the storeroom. Beyond it was the infirmary and I watched as Akira and his wife walked slowly out. They leaned heavily on each other as they took a short walk in the courtyard, trying to build their strength and breathe in the fresh mountain air. As they turned toward the storeroom, I stepped back, out of the light. I did not want them to see me. Everything about this felt wrong.

Can this be right? I thought. *Should I wear the clothes of the privileged while others starve?* I turned into the room and snatched a bolt of silk out of my sister's hands, throwing it back into the crate.

"While we play at dressing up, people are dying!" I said, no longer willing to keep my emotions bottled inside. "We should be out there—fighting Uncle!" Mother's lips set in a thin line, scoring her face. She came toward me and rescued the silk that I had thrown away. She held it up in front of me.

"We are not playing," she said, her voice cold. "But the time for swords and bloodshed is behind us." She smoothed down the hem of my kimono. "These are the threads you were born to wear, Kimi. You are the daughter of a *Jito*—and should behave accordingly."

I could say nothing more. I knew it would be too much for me to continue fighting my mother with words. My fingers twisted in the heavy silk of my obi sash. I stared hard at the ground and waited for my breathing to calm down. When I finally looked up, Mother was back at Hana's side, talking quietly to her. Then she turned to me.

"I have decided," she said. "Hana and you are to sell your swords. It will help to pay for a wig that you can wear at the wedding. The ladies of the court won't be used to the sight of such injuries on noble girls; the shock could be unpleasant for them. Hana can cover her arms, but it will be more difficult for you, Kimi." Behind her, Hana nodded in agreement.

I couldn't believe it. How did they think I could live without my sword? How did they think *they* could live without my sword? We may as well bare our necks to Uncle Hidehira and ask him to slash our throats—it was suicide.

"No," I whispered. My anger boiled up inside me and filled my voice with thunder. "No!" I said again. This time my shout echoed off the walls. This was too far. I could no longer bear the dark, musty oppression of the storeroom. I ran to the door. "I won't let you!" Then I plunged out into the light. My sword lay, glistening, on a low bench where I had left it that morning. I snatched it up and ran far from the store-room. Then I slashed the blade through the air. I would not be parted from my sword.

Not while Uncle was still alive.

CHAPTER THIRTEEN

I ran to a corner of the courtyard, where the thick trunk of an oak tree might hide me from observers. I tightened my grip around the hilt and lifted the blade above my head. I sliced across my phantom opponent—my uncle—and let the sword's momentum turn me around. I sliced again, more fiercely this time, but stumbled to the left and the smooth thrust of my sword turned jagged in the air. I would be dead by now in a real fight. But I didn't care. I raised my blade again and again. Sweat prickled my brow and the hilt slipped between my fingers, but I refused to pause in my exertions. *I must have my sword!* I told myself. *Ready to defeat any enemy.* Whenever I thought about abandoning my sword—for a *wig!*—fury rose up in me again and I brought my weapon around in loose blows. I was losing control of my technique, and I knew it. Blood pounded in my ears as I thought about all the fighting that lay before me. I could not abandon my sword; the sword was an extension of myself.

The tip of my sword grazed the ground and I found myself falling onto my knees, my head sinking against my chest. My fingers loosened and the sword fell quietly beside me.

A footfall sounded and I twisted around to see Daisuke emerge from behind the tree trunk. He came to kneel beside me on the gravel and gazed out over the monastery gardens toward the other side of the courtyard where monks were tending herbs.

"It seems you are still struggling with your anger, my friend," Daisuke said. Frustration boiled over in me again, and I wanted to bolt away. Daisuke reached out and touched my arm, calming me. He sat with me for a moment like that, waiting for me to speak.

"Mother wants Hana and me to sell our swords. To buy me"—I could barely spit out the words—"a wig."

My friend pointed at one of the monks. "That monk is one of our greatest fighters," he said. "There is no sword in his sash."

The man didn't look like a great fighter. His hair was gray and spare and I could see a slight paunch as he leaned over the herb bed, turning the soil.

Daisuke went on, "He is responsible for the security of this monastery. Without him, we would have fled long ago or been conquered." I frowned, still unable to see beyond the monk's shabby, graceless appearance. "He does not rely only on his sword, as you can see. He also has the keenest eyes of any of us and the sharpest brain. He fights best up here." Daisuke tapped a temple. "And here." He tapped his heart. "You could do the same, Kimi."

I thought hard about what Daisuke just said. "Are you saying I don't need my sword?" I asked hesitantly.

Daisuke nodded. "Say your good-byes, Kimi. You have a *new* fight ahead of you—one that will call on your sharp mind."

I scrambled to my feet to stand before Daisuke. I hesitated before saying what I really felt. "But how?" I asked, kicking the gravel. "I know how to use a sword. But how do I fight with my thoughts?" Daisuke climbed to his feet and looked at me, his silhouette blocking out the sun. The shadow of leaves from the tree danced across his face.

"You have to unite the noble families of Kamakura behind your cause. You already have the support of the people in the villages—now you must go to court and persuade the higher families to join forces against your enemy, for he is the enemy of all. For this, the sword is useless. You need strong words."

I gazed out one last time at the herb garden. The monk without a sword was climbing awkwardly to his feet, holding a hand to the small of his back. He leaned back, stretching stiff limbs, looking like an old man. But as he stretched, I noticed the way that his eyes scanned the horizon and his nostrils flared as he sniffed the air. He turned to a second monk and whispered something to him. I could see that Daisuke was right. A good fighter did not use his sword alone; he also used his mind. Father had once called it the strongest weapon of all.

Daisuke held out my sword.

I shook my head. "You keep it," I said.

He nodded at me, and I knew he understood that I would rather the sword be kept in the hand of a worthy warrior than be sold so that I could buy a *wig*.

I turned back to the storeroom to greet my mother and sister as they emerged from the low doorway. It was time to get ready. It was time to leave the monastery.

The next day dawned with a clear blue sky and crisp air. It was perfect weather for traveling. Mother gently shook me awake and I watched as she padded over to my brother's bed. Servants came into the room carrying a heavy tray with a round pot of green tea and small drinking bowls. As I poured the tea, my mother and sister dressed and Moriyasu scrambled into his clothes. I gazed around the room that had borne witness to our injuries and our healing. Would we ever see it again?

Mother held out the luxurious green kimono from yesterday.

"It's time, Kimi," she said. I took a last sip of the fragrant tea and walked over to have the cool silk draped around my shoulders. Hana already looked glorious in her robes. The silk rippled around her limbs as she lifted a hand to adjust the comb in her hair. She was everything she had been born to be— graceful, beautiful, and noble.

Hana caught my glance. "Look at me!" she said. "Can you believe I ever passed as a *boy*?"

I shook my head sadly. Our struggles together, escaping Uncle, disguised as boys, seemed a lifetime ago. Hana was a different person now. So was I, and I felt awkward and foolish in this costume.

Mother was adjusting the sash around her waist; she looked up and scrutinized each of her children in turn. She wiped the sleep from Moriyasu's eyes and shook her head indulgently.

"You'll do," she said. Then she glanced over at a box on the floor. A rigid wig of thick, black hair sat inside. A messenger had brought it for me yesterday evening and so far I had done my best to ignore it. Now I could escape it no longer. Mother picked up the wig and walked toward me, raising it into the air above my head. She paused.

"Ready to look beautiful again, Kimi?" she asked.

I nodded and tried to smile. Mother brought the wig down and adjusted it over my ears. I could feel the canvas scratching against my tender scalp and the thick, dark hair poked at my temples. My whole head started to itch, and I had to resist the urge to tear it off. Mother held up a small bronze mirror in front of Hana and me.

I did not recognize the two girls who gazed back at us. One wore a pretty smile while the other looked miserable, like someone wearing another person's clothes. I pulled at the wig to straighten it and tried to paint a smile on my face. Now the unhappy girl's face looked wretched. I saw Hana's smile falter and I turned away.

"The monks must be waiting for us," I announced as I strode toward the door and slid it open. "Let's say our good-byes."

Moriyasu ran ahead of us, as we three—a mother and her two daughters—made our way to the outer courtyard.

As we turned out of the doorway, Hana put a hand on my arm. "Are you all right, Kimi?" she asked. I nodded. What else could I do? I knew Hana wouldn't want to hear the truth. The last thing I wanted to do was steal her smile—not when she had been without it for so long. "You look beautiful," she added.

As we stepped out into the courtyard, a breath

caught in my throat. The monks had formed two rows, leading up to the monastery gates. They had all come out to bid us farewell. But not only the monks. I could see that some of the strongest from the infirmary had come out into the sunshine to say good-bye. The little girl and boy that Moriyasu had befriended raced over to greet us, their legs thin but strong. The little girl flung her arms around my brother, while the boy tugged on the hem of my sleeve.

"Are you off for more fighting, Kimi?" he asked eagerly.

I looked awkwardly at Mother. I glanced back down at the boy—so recently at death's door, now the color flooding his cheeks. I shook my head. "No," I said. "No more fighting. We go to court now."

The boy's face clouded. "What's that on your head?" he asked.

For the first time in days, a laugh erupted from me. "A wig!" I told him. "You should try one, it would suit you."

The boy shook his head vehemently. "No, thanks!" he said, racing back to Master Satoshi.

I smiled to watch him—it was good to see the children looking so healthy again. Moriyasu chased after the boy and tried to shove his small wooden *bokken* into the boy's hands. This *bokken* was my brother's favorite toy, and I had struggled through many difficult times carrying it with me, vowing to reunite him with it. I was filled with pride at the sight of him, so ready to sacrifice his favorite thing in the world for the happiness of another.

The boy shook his head and solemnly pushed the *bokken* back at Moriyasu. My brother smiled and bowed at the boy; they spoke for a brief moment, both nodding with what looked like determination. Then Moriyasu ran back to our side. "I wanted him to be able to protect his family," he explained.

"What did he say?" I asked.

"That it was more important for me to protect mine," my brother replied.

We walked toward the open gates of the monastery. Warrior monks stood guard, their swords by their side. As we walked past, each monk bowed his head in farewell. Eventually there was only one monk left—Daisuke. He stepped out and glanced in turn at each of us.

"You have been very special guests," he said. I felt as though my heart would break. Would Daisuke ever know how special he had become to us . . . to me? Mother took a step forward.

"We can never thank you for everything you have done for us. Hana's scars are healing. Kimi's hair is growing back. We are all still alive. But now we must go and seek justice," she said.

Daisuke nodded. "We understand. And Master Satoshi has asked me to tell you that we all wish you well in your cause." From the folds of his robes he pulled out a small box of polished wood. He came toward me and held it out.

"For you, Kimi," he said. I looked up, surprised, and took the box from him. I could see that it was hinged and when I opened up the honey-hued wood there was a miniature Go board and pieces inside. "Practice well and often," Daisuke continued. "And perhaps one day the two of us will play a game together again."

"Thank you," I whispered.

"I look forward to hearing about the rest of your long life—about the girl who once followed me through a waterfall," he said. Before I could reply, Mother was calling out to us.

"Come, girls," she was saying.

"One last thing," Daisuke said, his eyes intense. "There is something my heart does not want to let go of." He directed his glance at the square of silk that I had knotted around my wrist. "Could I?"

My hair was growing strongly, and now that I had a wig to wear I didn't need the scarf. I knew this was Daisuke's way of saying that he really cared. Smiling, I slid the silk off my arm and handed it over to Daisuke.

"Don't let Master Satoshi see," I teased.

Daisuke slipped the silk into the sleeve of his robe. "Good-bye, Kimi."

"Come, girls!" Mother called again. "Come, Moriyasu! It's time to go."

We climbed into our sidesaddles with Moriyasu in a man's saddle, and our horses pranced eagerly out of the courtyard. I glanced behind me one last time to see the heavy wooden gates of the monastery close. We were outsiders once more.

Then we turned to the path that wound down the mountain. Two of the warrior monks were escorting us and would return to the monastery with the horses we were borrowing.

I urged my horse on and began my descent down the mountain. I did not know what lay before me, but I knew that behind me I had left a friend.

I could only hope that we would meet again.

CHAPTER FOURTEEN

Our journey to Kamakura took us through dense, sloping forests. The horses struggled with the steep descent and we had to take regular breaks to rest their legs. The warrior monks scanned the trees, keeping an eye out for attackers.

"Come on!" Moriyasu called excitedly. "We have two days of riding ahead of us." His voice echoed off the trees of the forest. I turned my horse around. My little brother was right; we had much ground to cover.

As we traveled, we noticed that there *were* people among the trees. But they were not the enemy; they were the starving. Families had retreated to the forests to scavenge and find shelter now that their villages had been robbed and razed to the ground by Uncle. I felt ashamed of the clothes on my back and my horse's polished saddle as we rode past. Wide eyes gazed up at us from families huddled among the roots of the trees.

We came across an orchard run wild where a boy was trying to scale an apricot tree to harvest some of the fruit. Anyone could see that the apricots weren't ripe yet, but the boy was determined. His knees were grazed from unsuccessful efforts to scale the knobbly trunk and it was painful to watch him fall to the ground yet again. He kneeled in the grass, his chest heaving as he tried to catch his breath. When he looked up at us, I heard Hana gasp at the dark circles under his eyes.

My little brother pulled up on his horse and leaped out of his saddle. He went over to the tree, one of the warrior monks following on his horse.

"Moriyasu!" Mother called after him. But it was too late; he had already unsheathed his *bokken*. The boy on the ground cringed away, backing up against the tree trunk and whimpering.

"Don't worry," Moriyasu said. "I only want to help." He raised his *bokken* into the air and pulled it back behind his head, before hurling it into the branches of the apricot tree. The wooden sword circled through the air, neatly knocking an apricot, which fell to the ground at the boy's feet. He pounced on the fruit and lifted the apricot to his mouth, biting fiercely into the hard flesh. He smiled as he chewed.

"Thank you," he said, gulping down a piece of apricot. "Who are you?"

143

Moriyasu looked back questioningly at the rest of us. Mother shook her head at him. "Just a boy," said Moriyasu, as he walked back to his horse. The warrior monks shared a glance.

As I guided my horse, I knew that Moriyasu wasn't just a boy. He was born to be a *Jito*, and I swore that one day he would be able to extend his generosity of spirit far over the land.

I'll make it happen, I told myself. *I have to.*

After a day and a half of traveling, we arrived at the gates of the Shogun's compound. It was time for the warrior monks to leave us. They helped us bring down our trunks and then bowed.

"Stay safe," said one of them.

Mother bowed her head in response. Moriyasu stood up in his stirrups and waved a fist in the air. "I'll take care of my family!" he cried.

I dipped my head to hide my smile but the monks' expressions remained serious. "We know you will," said one of them as the other gathered up our horses' reins. "Farewell."

The wooden gates of the compound reared up before us. Across the front walls of the compound ran a moat—I kneeled down to run my fingers through the cool water. As I brought handfuls of water up to my face, I caught my reflection in the moat. My wig had slipped and I could see the streak of white in my hair. I tugged the wig back into place.

As I got back to my feet, Hana called over to me and I turned around to see two guards watching us. Fear prickled my skin as I noticed the vicious glitter of their swords. My hand went to my side, but too late I remembered that my sword was back at the monastery. Mother walked over the wooden bridge, approaching one of the guards. She held out the scroll of paper that invited us to the Administrator's wedding.

The guard glanced at the scroll and then banged a fist against the gates. With a heavy grind, they began to part—dragged open by servants on the other side of the compound's walls.

"Are you frightened, Kimi?" Hana asked me, as our footsteps crunched in the gravel. I knew those giveaway sounds were there to alert the inhabitants of the compound to any unwelcome visitors.

My heart beat loudly in my chest, though I knew that we had every right to be here.

"Only a little," I told Hana. I had no idea what was waiting for us. But from the heavy scent of incense on the air, I knew it would be formal and impressive. *You're the daughter of a Jito,* I reminded myself. I knew how to behave. But as I glanced down at the rough calluses that covered my hands, I wondered if the court was ready for *me*. I pulled my hands behind my back and waited alongside my family for the doors to the inner compound to be heaved open by another set of servants.

The doors opened, and we stepped into the courtyard as a group of ladies walked past, huddled together and whispering behind their fans. In one corner of the courtyard was a pond garden, with low benches. Councillors and their wives strolled through the garden, beneath the nut trees.

Some servants carried flower arrangements toward the main compound, while others brushed leaves out of the courtyard.

"Those tables are used at wedding feasts," Mother whispered to us. "Preparations for the wedding must be in hand."

A tall man with gray hair approached us and gave a short bow.

"We welcome the Yamamoto family," he said. "The Administrator is expecting you. Please—follow me. I will show you to your apartments. The wedding reception will take place shortly, and you may want to change." His glance traveled over my wig and I felt my cheeks blush hot.

Mother led the way behind the man, and Hana and I followed. Moriyasu brought up the rear with none of his usual exuberance. We walked across the courtyard, and people turned to watch us pass. A young woman lifted an ornate fan to her face so that all I could see of her was her wide eyes following me. Then she leaned over to whisper to her companion, who laughed quietly. I could see that groups of people were whispering and muttering to each other again. I was no fool; I recognized the sound of scandal. Our story had already reached these privileged ears. They were gossiping about a family without a father, turned out by their uncle. I continued walking, desperate to escape this inspection. I folded my hands in front of me and prayed that no one would notice how rough the skin was. But Hana's head was held high.

I should be strong, too, I thought. Whatever these people had to say, I could not allow their malice to divert me from my purpose: to meet the Shogun and persuade him to fight on our side.

As we turned into a cool walkway, my shoulders sagged.

"What a torture!" I whispered to Hana, but she did not reply. She was stepping into our apartment with shining eyes. She swirled around, taking in the luxurious surroundings.

Thick tatami mats covered the floor, and the windows of the apartment were opaque—no one could see in or out. A bronze vase sat on a low blackwood table, holding a single orchid, and in one corner of the large room stood a folding screen, on which painted cranes took flight across its surface. Even our rooms at home had not been this opulent.

Soon Hana was lifting a fresh kimono out of our luggage, brought through by servants. She held the outfit up before her, a silk of chrysanthemum colors. She climbed into the undergarment of deep red and Mother held out an obi sash embroidered with silver thread in a pattern of butterflies and birds. She pushed a comb into her thick hair and glanced up at me. Her cheeks flushed red with excitement.

"A wedding, Kimi!" she said. "How long since we attended one of those?" I could see how happy she was to be here, but couldn't bring myself to feel the same.

Moriyasu stood by the door, his hand resting on the handle of his *bokken*. He was keeping guard. All of a sudden, my little brother seemed to be growing up.

"Come on, Kimi," Mother chided. "Everything we do here will be under scrutiny. We must impress if we are to win over the Shogun. We mustn't keep the Administrator waiting."

I hurried to the luggage and pulled out a tangerine kimono with a pale green undergarment. Mother tweaked and smoothed as I dressed myself in the

148

glossy silk. I adjusted the wig on my head and turned to my family.

"Will I do?" I asked.

Tears lit up Mother's eyes. She nodded once, deeply. "I am so proud of you all."

"Let's go!" Hana said. My throat tightened as I watched my excited sister sweep past me. She hurried out of the door and onto the walkway, not looking back.

Mother rested a hand on my shoulder. "Ready?" she asked gently.

I nodded stiffly. Then I followed my family out.

As we walked into the main hall, crowds of people had already gathered. Folding screens broke the room up, allowing people to gather in smaller groups. Around the room, screens had been pulled back to allow a view of the garden outside.

The air was heavy with scent from the perfumed robes. Painted silks, mother-of-pearl fans, and men with ornate swords surrounded us. Hana's eyes scanned the room eagerly, taking in all the sights. I could only look at the raised platform at the front of the room where a man kneeled, poised and strong. Behind him were screens that I knew would be hiding guards. This was the Shogun—the man I had heard so much about. He wore a beard and mustache, and had wide cheekbones and a full mouth that turned down slightly at the corners. It was impossible to tell what he was thinking. The Shogun's black robes glistened like ebony in the light from the lamps and I could see the ornate, curved sword that rested by his side. His well-oiled hair was piled high on his head and in one hand he held a fan.

Behind him sat an older woman who shared the same wide cheekbones. His mother, I guessed. She sat with her back held rigidly straight, despite her years, and looked out with piercing eyes. She had broad shoulders, and age had given her a vivid, white streak through her hair, just like mine.

I walked through the crowd, being careful not to step on anyone's hem. As I approached, I could see the Shogun gazing around the room, taking everything in. The servant who had welcomed us to the compound whispered something into the Shogun's ear before indicating with a nod of his head toward the crowd. Some message about guests? It was too much to hope that he was telling the Shogun of our arrival; I knew we were not significant.

Through the crowd, my eyes met the Shogun's. His gaze was steady and I steeled myself to hold it. The sounds of the hall fell away and suddenly I felt as though the two of us were the only people in the room. As I gazed at the Shogun, I could see that he was everything I strived to be—calm, composed, certain. For the first time, I allowed myself to truly believe that Mother could be right. Perhaps this man *could* help us.

I took another step forward—did I dare approach the Shogun now? But a uniformed guard stepped up onto the platform. He wore the embroidered uniform of a samurai at a formal ceremony and walked with the light step of a young, strong man. As he kneeled down to speak quietly to the Shogun, I thought I saw something familiar in his stance. The guard turned to scrutinize the crowds. As his gaze ranged across the gathered faces, I felt the hair on the nape of my neck stiffen. This was a face I had never expected to see here, in the Shogun's compound. This young man was dressed in the most prestigious uniform of a Shogun samurai. He was also our friend.

It was Tatsuya.

CHAPTER FIFTEEN

I glanced around the room, looking for Hana. She was bowing her head respectfully as an older woman admired her outfit. I pushed through the crowd and grabbed Hana's arm.

"Kimi! You're hurting me!" she gasped, pulling away. I had momentarily forgotten about her burns.

Hana turned away from me, rubbing her arm. "I am sorry," she said to the woman. "My sister is so excited to be attending the wedding." I stared at Hana, amazed to hear her apologizing for me. The woman glanced at me.

"No need to apologize," she said. But she was already backing away from us, looking for someone else to talk to. *Someone with a better sense of etiquette,* I thought bitterly.

I brought my face close to Hana's ear.

"Look over at the Shogun's platform," I whispered. Hana shrugged.

"The entire room is looking at the Shogun," she

said. "You pushed through the crowds to tell me that?"

I couldn't help the impatient tut that escaped me. "Look at the soldier guarding him," I said. I watched Hana's face as she scrutinized the warrior. Slow seconds passed and I saw the blood gradually fade from her flushed cheeks as realization dawned. She swallowed hard.

"Is it . . . ?" she began. Then she tore her glance away from the stage, staring at the floor. "I can hardly believe it is true," she said. She looked up at me, her eyes searching my face for the answer.

A smile broke out over my face. "It is true," I said. "It's Tatsuya. Hana—he's alive!"

People were pushing past us for a better position by the raised platform; it was becoming difficult to see our friend through the throng. Hana abandoned any sense of decorum. She grabbed my hand fiercely and pulled me to the edge of the room.

The crowd was thinner here and we followed the wall down toward the platform. Tatsuya was on the stage, above us, gazing out over the crowds, his face serious and his mouth set firm.

I remembered the first time we had met Tatsuya in Master Goku's school—his pleasant face and short black hair. His eyes were the same now as they had been back then—dark and unreadable. But other things had changed. His body was bigger beneath the panels of his uniform and his stance had turned aggressive. Our friend was a soldier now—how had this happened?

Tatsuya must have sensed our gaze on him. He looked down at us and I could see him frown in confusion and then his eyes widen. The last time Tatsuya had seen us we had worn the topknots and rough garb of peasant boys; now we were adorned in the splendor of noble women. We must have looked very different, but he recognized us.

Beside me, Hana gazed up at Tatsuya, smiling widely. Her chest heaved as she struggled to contain her emotions, and I hoped that Hana would not give herself away. We could not afford for anyone to notice that we knew Tatsuya—how would we explain all of our adventures together, fighting side by side? People clearly knew that we had been ousted by our uncle— the whole province knew that—but what would they think if they knew Hana and I had been forced to disguise ourselves as boys, or that we had felt the blood of battle on our hands?

"Soldier!" the white-haired man called out. "We have need of your sword." Tatsuya glanced around to see a woman standing beside the platform, her kimono trailing a long silken thread. She giggled behind her fan as she held out the thread. Tatsuya marched over and unsheathed his sword, holding it up in the light of the lamps. Impressed gasps could be heard among the crowd. Then Tatsuya kneeled awkwardly in his uniform and brought the blade of his sword through the loose thread.

"Thank you," the lady said, allowing the thread to fall into Tatsuya's open palm. He said nothing as he stood back up and sheathed his sword. A warrior brought to his knees to play dressmaker. It didn't seem right. Not for my friend. But his position would also bring him status, something he did not have before.

"We must speak to him in private," Hana whispered to me, her breath hot on my cheek. "I can't wait!"

Behind us, the crowd fell silent and Tatsuya looked over our heads at the back of the room. I swiveled around in time to see the bride and her new husband enter the main hall. The bride ducked her head modestly and hid her face behind a large, white fan. Mother-of-pearl picked out details in the fan, shining in the lamplight. The bride's hair was hidden beneath a large headdress, and she wore a brocaded kimono that hung from her shoulders in heavy folds.

"So modest and beautiful," Hana breathed, as we hurried back to Mother's side.

The Administrator led his new wife around the

room, greeting guests. He stood tall and I noticed the way he smiled at each person in turn, finding a few polite words for everyone. When an elderly woman was too frail to stand up from her seat, he was happy to squat and share a few moments with her. *A kind man, then,* I thought. I hoped this boded well for our cause.

"He's so handsome!" a young woman gushed from behind her fan. I bit my lip to stop the laugh that threatened to erupt. The silliness! Was this what the Shogun's court was about?

Hana nudged me, and I saw that the bride and groom were approaching us. The bride smiled at Mother and for the first time I noticed that behind the meekness, there was a light playing in this woman's eyes. She lowered her fan so that her voice could be heard by everyone.

"I have heard much of your plight," she said. People gasped—this was the first time anyone had acknowledged out loud what had happened to my family. "And you have my every sympathy," the bride continued. "I am glad to see you here today and I hope that some of our small happiness will lighten your own heart. You have suffered much and deserve the gods to smile on you again." Then she bowed to Mother and to little Moriyasu.

Now it was my turn to gasp. I knew what an honor

this was—for the wife of the Administrator to bow to another woman at her own wedding reception. As the bride straightened up, I could see her watching Mother's face keenly. Mother dipped her head in acknowledgment. I could sense everyone waiting to hear what she'd say.

"The gods have already smiled on us by bringing us here to your wedding." This was the perfect thing to say. Mother had acknowledged our heartache, without dwelling on it—and she had managed to turn the conversation into a compliment to the married couple.

Beside me, Hana smiled. "We must be certain of success now," she whispered.

People were turning to look at us with a new light in their eyes—interest and curiosity. Before, people had whispered behind their fans; now I sensed the crowd drawing closer around us. Thanks to the Administrator's wife, we were no longer a scandal. From his place on the stage, the Shogun watched. His expression had not changed.

The Administrator helped his bride step up onto the raised platform and they kneeled down beside the Shogun. Tatsuya was still on the edge of the stage, keeping guard. Mother led us to a low table and we joined the rest of the diners as the celebratory meal began. Moriyasu's stomach grumbled loudly and he smiled broadly.

"My belly has not discovered its manners yet," he apologized to the other diners. People laughed indulgently and Hana and I shared a secret, delighted glance. Our brother was already charming the powerful families of Kamakura.

We settled down to the meal. Dish after dish was brought out—sliced raw tuna on a bed of seaweed, clear soup in lacquered bowls, pickled ginger, roasted gingko nuts. Pale green tea was poured into our porcelain cups and pounded rice cakes sat, waiting to be eaten. As I reached out for a bowl of steamed rice, I thought about our time hiding in the innkeeper's hut and our modest daily meals of miso soup and scraps of food. I thought about the people I had met in Daisuke's infirmary—the sick and starving. My stomach turned over and my appetite disappeared. I pushed my food away, but Mother looked up sharply and I realized that politeness obliged me to eat. I picked up my chopsticks and lifted a shred of dried cucumber to my lips, forcing myself to chew and swallow. All around me, faces shone greasily as men and women devoured the delicacies placed before them. This wedding feast was an insult to starving people all over the estates.

As the meal drew to a close, a message was sent from the bride, asking Hana to recite a poem.

Another honor! But the two of us had spent so many days away from any type of noble life—would she be able to remember the poems we had recited as children?

Hana cleared her throat and she began. A hush fell over the room as her delicate voice rang off the walls and filled the air. The poem she recited was one I knew well. It was written in our grandmother's diary, and Hana and I had learned it by heart long ago. It was a poem about two lovers, the man promising he would return as the plum tree blossomed:

> Wait on, never forsake your hope,
> For when the azalea is in flower
> Even the unpromised, the unexpected, will come
> to you.

As the poem came to an end, Hana gazed across the room toward the raised platform. The crowds must have thought Hana was looking over at the Administrator and his bride. I knew better; her glance was for Tatsuya.

Through the window behind Hana, I could see an azalea in the courtyard dip and bow in the cool breeze, its petals falling gently to the ground. As Hana took her seat, my eyes brimmed with tears. I gazed over at our friend on the other side of the room. The unexpected had indeed arrived. Tatsuya was still alive and he was here—in this very room.

I turned to see Moriyasu laughing and joking as he taught another boy the rules of Go. Mother conversed quietly with a woman sitting next to her, while Hana happily recited more poems for the people sitting around her. My family was in their element, charming our new acquaintances.

Beneath the table, my fingers twisted in my lap. *I can't do this,* I thought. I did not possess the easy charm of my sister and brother, nor the expert confidence of my mother. I had spent too many days living in woods and being hunted. How could I pretend to be carefree now? And at the back of my mind was always the one thought—*Uncle.* What was he doing now? As we sat here, how many were suffering on his orders?

A woman came to sit beside me. Her back was bowed and her face was pinched, as though she had spent a lifetime grimacing at unpleasant thoughts. She leaned across the table toward my mother and interrupted her conversation.

"By whose invitation are you here?" she asked sharply. Mother glanced up, shocked. Then she managed to compose herself and allowed her expression to soften.

"By invitation from the Administrator," she said. "Yourself?"

The woman cleared her throat. "The same," she said, looking away. Then she darted a second accusatory glance at Mother. "And your rooms—are they sufficient for a short stay? Have they given you bedrolls?" Mother's face creased in a frown, and I could tell she wondered the same thing I did: Why was this woman throwing such direct questions at her?

"Our beds are most adequate," Mother said, "and we have an open invitation to stay. Our rooms are beautiful and we are extremely honored." The woman folded her arms beneath her bust and shrugged.

"Your husband died attacking his brother, did he not? Should a widow be out traveling alone to get here? Perhaps it would have been better for you to miss the wedding reception."

My mother's face flushed red and I found myself turning to the woman. Hana shot me a warning glance but it was too late. I would not allow my mother to be insulted like this. It was time to use strong words.

"It is in our father's memory that we are here," I said, trying to control the tremble in my voice. "He was an honorable man who attacked no one, much less his own brother. Shame on you for spreading lies."

The woman struggled to her feet and I held out no hand to help her. "I can't help what people say," she mumbled. Then she walked toward the doors of the hall, leaving the party. She had shamed herself and she knew it.

I watched her leave through narrowed eyes, and then turned back to Mother. "So much for the politeness of privilege," I said. I stood up from the tatami mat. The Shogun had already left the room and it was in order for others to retire now if they chose to. I was breaking no rules of conduct.

"Where are you going, Kimi?" Mother asked. Her voice was strained and I could see that the efforts of the afternoon had taken their toll on her. But I had to get out—I had to get away from here.

"I need some fresh air," I said. "I feel faint."

The woman sitting beside Mother turned at these words. "A stroll outside will make you feel better," she said.

I thanked her and turned toward the doors of the hall.

"Wait, Kimi. I'll come with you and make sure you're all right," Hana said, scrambling to her feet.

"Such a kind girl. And so beautiful," I heard the woman murmur to our mother.

Hana and I walked out of the hall and once we were on the walkway, Hana whispered, "We can go in search of Tatsuya now." Our friend had left with the Shogun and could be anywhere in the compound.

Two guards marched past us and Hana and I exchanged a glance.

"They could lead us to the soldiers' quarters," I said. "Tatsuya might be there."

Hana squeezed my arm. "Then, let's follow!"

Now that I was out of the main hall, I could feel my spirits returning. We turned and followed the guards, padding softly.

The two men marched down the walkway and turned sharply at the corner. We waited for a moment and then chased after them. Walkways led off the galleried rooms and we found ourselves being led farther and farther away from the main hall and into the darker rooms occupied by servants and soldiers. We were far away from our quarters, but our time at Master Goku's had made us familiar with kitchens and servants' rooms.

"This would have terrified us once upon a time," I whispered to Hana. Wealthy girls were not allowed to roam unaccompanied.

She smiled. "What fools we were back then," she agreed. It was a relief to know that Hana still remembered what we had been through, despite the finery of the clothes we now wore.

But as we turned a corner, we lost the soldiers. I tried to retrace our steps but the corridor behind us split off at several points and I could not remember which way we had come. I turned back to my sister, her face puzzled.

"You know what we've done, don't you?" I asked. Hana shook her head uncertainly. "One day of wearing fine kimonos and our minds have turned to mush. Hana—we're lost!"

CHAPTER SIXTEEN

T he sound of marching feet rang off the floorboards, and Hana pulled me back against
a wall. We hid in the deep shadows of the
walkway and waited for two new soldiers to march
past, their heads held high and proud. We followed
them for a few moments, but then they turned down
a busy walkway and we had to pull back. We pinned
ourselves against a wall again.

"What now?" Hana asked. As she spoke, we heard
male voices ringing out from a building across the
small courtyard.

"That could be the soldiers' quarters," I whispered
to Hana. I strode toward the building, determined to
find our friend, but Hana pulled me back. "What is
it?" I asked. "What's wrong?"

"Look at us." Hana swept a hand over the rich silk
of her kimono. "We are the daughters of a high family. We can't be discovered among soldiers in their
own quarters. It would be a scandal." I had to admit,

Hana had a point. But frustration simmered inside me—*why* couldn't we go where we liked? Being back among polite society had made me half the girl I once was.

Another soldier strode up to the door.

"Are you lost?" he asked, when he saw us. "Should I escort you back to the main hall?" He towered above us, but his eyes shone kindly. I decided to take a chance.

"Please," I said, "can you help us? We have reason to believe that an old friend of ours is a samurai in your quarters. His name is Tatsuya." I saw the glimmer of recognition in the soldier's eyes. "Do you think you could persuade him to step outside and exchange a few words with us? It would mean so much." I waited for the soldier's response, my heart beating strongly in my chest. Either he would help us or he would march us straight back to the main hall.

The man smiled. "Oh, I know Tatsuya. He's fast become the Shogun's favorite—and ours. I'll find him for you and *order* him to come out here to see you!" My shoulders sagged with relief. The soldier turned to the heavy doorway, but I put out a hand. He looked down at me in surprise.

"Please," I said. "Don't tell anyone we were here."

The man glanced around him, as though looking for someone. "I don't know what you mean," he said.

"I haven't seen a soul down here. Certainly there's been no sign of two finely dressed girls."

I smiled widely and glanced over at Hana, who couldn't mask her own grin.

The door closed behind the soldier and we heard gruff shouts across the room. A moment later, the door heaved open.

There stood Tatsuya. He wore the simple trousers and tunic of a soldier at rest. But his sword remained in its hilt by his side—always on duty. He looked over his shoulder and then stepped out into the walkway, pulling the door shut behind him.

"Tatsuya, what happened to you?" Hana asked. "The last time we saw you, you were being captured! We thought . . ." She did not dare voice that darkest thought.

Tatsuya's face clouded at the sight of Hana's emotion. "I'm alive—even if we haven't seen each other for an age." He looked us up and down, taking in our fine kimonos. "And you look much different from when I last saw you. Where are your swords?"

My smile faltered. "We no longer carry swords," I said quietly. But now was no time for regret. There were too many questions. "What are you doing here?" I asked. "And how did you escape the ninja?"

"Did you know we would be here?" Hana asked excitedly, drawing close to Tatsuya.

At the mention of ninja, Tatsuya looked nervously along the walkway and put a finger to his lips. "Shush," he said. "This is not a good place to talk. Let's go out to the pond garden, where there is no hiding place for spies."

"Spies?" I asked.

"You know, eavesdroppers," he replied. "Samurai soldiers are as bad as old women for sniffing out gossip. Come on." He turned and led us down a walkway.

The pond garden was empty—most guests would be sleeping off the lavish feast by now. Five ponds were fed by a stream that flowed from one to the other. A weeping willow tree trailed its leaves in the largest of the ponds and we ducked between the long, flowing branches to sit hidden from the rest of the compound. The ground was mossy and Hana and I sat on either side of Tatsuya on a low bench.

"Tell us your story. From the very beginning," said Hana.

Tatsuya took a deep breath. "When the ninja dragged me out of the river, I thought I was going to die."

I remembered the ninja attack on the monastery and how Daisuke and I had battled those silent assassins and their ruthless determination. I could imagine the fear that must have been pounding through Tatsuya's heart.

"Why didn't they kill you?" Hana asked.

"I don't know," he said. "They knocked me out and put me in a cell. I managed to escape—"

"How?" I interrupted. I could not understand how these trained men had allowed our friend to slip from their grasp. *Tatsuya must be more of a warrior than I realized,* I thought. But he waved a dismissive hand through the air.

"I escaped when they brought me some food," he said. "Two ninja gave chase and I really thought I would meet my death." I opened my mouth to ask another question, but Tatsuya pushed on, determined that no one would interrupt him this time. "Ninja are effective because they rely on the element of surprise in their attack. But I *knew* they were chasing me, so I was prepared. I still had my bow and arrow, so I scrambled up a tree and . . ." He mimed the action of pulling the bow taut and releasing an arrow. "One! Two! One in the heart, the other straight through his eyeball and into his head. I didn't try to retrieve *that* arrow!" Tatsuya leaned back and folded his arms, proud of his story.

But Hana's face had turned ghostly white. "To die like that," she said quietly. She shuddered and Tatsuya's arms fell to his side.

"A villager gave me food," he continued, changing

the subject, "and a bed. He told me that the Shogun was looking for new recruits. So I came here and won a place."

"But the Shogun chooses his men from the best dojo in the land. How did you get an audience with him?" I was amazed that it could be so easy.

Tatsuya's face hardened. "I used my fighting skills to impress one of the samurai captains and then won my place. You do remember Master Goku's training—don't you?" Sarcasm flooded his voice and I could see that our friend was annoyed by all my questions. It seemed his new status as a Shogun's samurai had gone to his head. I had seen Tatsuya's anger before when I had teased him about imaginary ninja, but I had never heard his voice take on such a hostile tone.

"Of course I remember," I said quietly. "And you were so kind to us then, too." I hoped my words would remind Tatsuya of our first meeting and our secret training sessions in his room. Of how much we had done together.

Tatsuya's hands had bunched into fists, but he relaxed them at the memory. "And you? What of you two?" he asked.

Hana and I glanced at each other. "We went on to fight Uncle Hidehira in the battle for the estate in Sagami," I explained. "We met a battalion of students who were willing to fight alongside us. We rescued

Mother and Moriyasu and escaped the fighting. Then, after weeks of hiding in villages, samurai soldiers arrived on Uncle's orders and—"

"We ended up hiding in a monastery," Hana interrupted.

I glanced over at her and she discreetly shook her head in my direction. I understood. Hana did not want Tatsuya to know about the fire—about her scars. Not yet, anyway. My scalp itched beneath my wig and I wondered if Tatsuya thought my headgear strange. I sympathized with Hana wanting to hide her scars.

I didn't have a chance to say anything else. The leaves of the willow tree were roughly pushed aside and three samurai soldiers stepped into the clearing beside the pond. Their armor glistened in the last rays of the setting sun.

"Hah!" one of them laughed. "Talking with girls. Well, well. Looks like Tatsuya isn't quite the soldier our Shogun thinks he is. Careful, Tatsuya. Your muscles will turn flabby if you sit here too long."

Tatsuya jerked up to his feet and brought his shoulders back rigidly. Looking straight ahead, he explained himself: "These are old friends from school. I would be rude to spurn their eagerness for news." I could see how hurt Hana was by Tatsuya's formal words and I suddenly hated the men for interrupting us. I scrambled to my feet, too.

"From school?" asked a second samurai. "You trained with girls?" All three of the men roared with vicious laughter. As one of them leaned back, throwing his face to the sky, I leaped behind him and unsheathed his long *daito* sword. It was heavier than any sword I had ever practiced with, but its layers of cold steel glistened in the sunlight. I heard Hana gasp in shock and Tatsuya call out to me to stop. But the hilt of the sword felt good in my hand and I already knew I was ready to fight.

I circled the man, enjoying his shocked expression.

"How dare you," he hissed. "No one robs a samurai of his sword."

"No samurai allows his sword to be taken," I said. "No *good* samurai, at least. You want to see how girls train with swords? I could beat you all!"

One of the soldiers took out a small *shoto* sword and threw it to the unarmed samurai. As the other two unsheathed their swords, I sprang forward and brought the flat of my blade down heavily on the first man's wrist. He cried out in pain and allowed the *shoto* sword to fall to the ground, where it speared the moss. I kicked the little sword aside and it plunged into the pond, disappearing beneath the rippling water. The second samurai brought his sword around above his

172

head in a two-handed grip and drew the blade down through the air. I jumped to the side, bringing up my own sword to deflect the blow. As I sliced up through the air, the third samurai attacked, lunging forward to bring his sword around in a strong, smooth strike toward my left side—my exposed heart. I swirled around and kept my arms straight in front of me. The tip of my sword grazed the man's chest and he jerked back, allowing his sword arm to fall. He stumbled over a tree root and fell to the ground.

I turned, ready for the next attack, my sword held out before me. My chest was heaving as I panted for air. One man was on his knees by the pond, trying to retrieve his sword. The other was watching me keenly, his own sword held out in front of him.

"You have spirit," he commented.

"Don't you want to fight on?" I asked.

He shook his head. "You are good. I apologize. But the best sword is the sheathed sword." He took a step backward and put his sword back in its sheath. "I'll see no blood spilled today."

I hesitated, then handed my sword back to its owner, hilt first. I had proved myself to these men and they would not make the mistake of laughing at me again. I turned around to Tatsuya, expecting to see how I had impressed him. After all, I had done a lot of fighting since we had last seen each other. I was sure my technique must have improved. But his mouth turned down at the corners and I could see that his hands had bunched into fists again. Behind him, Hana watched—her face pale and anxious.

"Get out of my way!" Tatsuya pushed past me, following the other soldiers back to their quarters.

"Tatsuya?" I called out uncertainly.

He swiveled around and marched back, bringing his face close to mine. "Don't you ever humiliate me like that again," he said. He was so close that I could see the spittle gathering in the corners of his mouth.

"But I was defending your honor," I said. "There's no shame in training with girls."

"When I want my honor saved, I'll save it myself. In the meantime, try not to show me up in front of the other soldiers. Keep your sword fighting for entertaining children at fancy parties."

One of the soldiers turned around from the other side of the courtyard. "That's some friend you have!" he called back jokingly to Tatsuya.

Tatsuya's eyes narrowed. "Some friend, indeed," he whispered menacingly. Then he turned on his heel and ran away across the gravel.

Hana came to stand beside me. "What have you done, Kimi?" she asked.

I shook my head. "I don't know," I said.

"Well, *I* know," said Hana. "All you ever want to do is fight. Why couldn't you have left Tatsuya to be teased by his friends? They meant no harm."

As I heard the door slam behind Tatsuya, I wondered what had happened to our friend during his imprisonment. What had made his gentle face contort in anger? Hana was wrong; it couldn't just be me. Something else had happened to Tatsuya—something bad.

I couldn't sleep that night. I tossed and turned under my heavy covers. I got up from my bed and dragged a cover after me to lie on the cool floor. For so long, I had slept on floorboards and now I could not sleep away from them. The scent of pine filled my nostrils and I lay on my back, gazing up toward the eaves of the room. My last waking thought was for Tatsuya. *May he sleep well,* I asked the gods. *And someday find the brightness he once had.* Whatever had happened to unsettle his soul, I hoped it would not keep him from his dreams.

CHAPTER SEVENTEEN

The next morning was spent quietly in our apartment. In the privacy of our rooms, I could abandon my wig and run my hands over the prickles of my cropped hair.

"We'll always be able to spot you in the courtyard," my brother joked with me, referring to my white streak.

Moriyasu and I played a game of Go, while Hana and Mother arranged our belongings around the room. Every now and then, I would look up from the polished game board that Daisuke had given me and gaze out of the window at a red maple tree. I thought about my friend often—what was he doing now? My thoughts chased one another back and forth, and it was no surprise to me that Moriyasu won the game.

"Concentrate, Kimi!" my brother chided me. I smiled as we put the pieces back in their bowls, ready for a new game.

There was a call from outside the door of the

apartment and a servant stepped into the room.

"What is it?" Mother asked, walking over from the mat where she had spread out our kimonos for inspection.

"I have a message from Lady Akane, wife of the Administrator," said the servant. "Please, would you join her in the Administrator's wing for tea and *ikebana* flower arranging? All the women are attending the *ikebana*, but Lady Akane would like to take tea with you first."

Mother's face flushed with pleasure and I heard Hana gasp in delight. Moriyasu rolled his eyes at me and I tried not to laugh.

"Flower arranging," he said. "I can hardly contain my excitement." I leaned across the board and pinched his cheek.

"It's okay for *you*," I whispered. "You won't be expected to go. Boys get all the luck in this world."

"That's right," Moriyasu said, nodding at the Go board. "Because we are the best strategists. You would do well to learn from me, sister." I lunged forward to pinch his cheek again—more fiercely this time—but Moriyasu was too quick for me and ducked past the servant to race out into the courtyard.

"Don't stray too far," Mother called after him.

The servant was still waiting for an answer.

"Please tell Lady Akane that we would be honored

to attend," said Mother. As the servant exited the room, Mother swirled around and clapped her hands together sharply.

"Come, girls." She held out my wig for me and I reluctantly put it on. Once it was on, Mother seemed satisfied. Hana adjusted her kimono and soon we were ready to depart.

Another servant had come to show us the way to Akane's apartments. We followed him down long walkways, through the main hall, and toward other rooms set apart in the compound. A simple doorway led into a room that was as wide as four tatami mats, gracefully lit by screened windows. We went in one by one and the fragrant scent of the straw mats filled the air. Opposite us was an alcove that contained a beautiful flower arrangement and a scroll that carried a poem about harmony and respect.

Mother herded Hana and me to a low table, where we kneeled to wait for Akane. I tried to convince myself that I didn't mind attending flower arranging. *Perhaps we can appeal to the Administrator's wife for support?* I thought.

A moment later, she came in through the doorway. She wore a simpler kimono today, but it was still beautiful—powder-blue silk with an ivory undergarment. The colors played well against the pale beauty of her skin—Akane clearly knew how to bring out her own best qualities.

"Do you think we could ever have such presence?" Hana whispered to me.

"With my hair?" I joked. Immediately I regretted it, as I saw Hana's hands move over her scars, even though they were safely covered from view by the folds of her kimono sleeves. Hana's injuries were still too raw for her to joke about.

"Good morning," Akane said, nodding at each of us in turn. As her gaze came to rest on my face, I bowed my head. But when I looked back up, Akane was still scrutinizing me. After a few heartbeats, she glanced one final time around the room and kneeled at a low table to prepare the tea.

As Akane's hands moved deftly, we all watched. Drinking tea was a moment of high ritual and I was interested to see how the Administrator's bride would perform. She sat with her legs folded under her, thighs parallel. Then she took a lacquered container and spooned green powder into a porcelain bowl, decorated in floral designs. She then ladled hot water into the bowl. Akane picked up a small bamboo whisk and turned over the water and leaves until the fragrant aroma of green tea filled the air. She bent over her work, steam rising up to her face as she poured the first cup of green tea, which she presented to Mother. She took a sip and Akane presented the next cup of tea to me, and then to Hana.

Akane's actions were economical and precise; no energy was wasted on exaggerated display or showy movements. I realized that behind the meekness of her bridal performance yesterday was a woman who was undoubtedly sure of herself. With the eyes of my family on her, she never once faltered.

"I know much of your husband's good work," Akane said to Mother. "And I was grieved by his death. When I heard of your letter, I was determined that you should all attend my wedding ceremony. I don't care what rumors some of the councillors' wives may spread. To my mind, you are a deserving family." I knew she must be referring to the rumor we had heard yesterday— that our father had launched an attack on Uncle and that he had died without honor.

Mother gently placed her cup of tea back down on the table. "We are forever in your debt," she said. "The kindness you have shown does much to heal the wounds left by my husband's death."

My impatience bubbled under the surface. All this talk of healing wounds and kindness was all very good, but Uncle was still out there rampaging across the territories. We needed strong words to save lives.

"Can you get us an audience with the Shogun?" I blurted out, putting my cup down with a clunk, disturbing the peaceful atmosphere.

"Kimi," Mother chided. She turned immediately to Akane. "I apologize. I hope no harm is done because of my daughter's clumsiness—or her boldness."

Akane's eyes were crinkled with amusement. Beyond her, the servant waited for orders and I could see his mouth twitch.

I'm a joke to these people, I realized, with a stab of shame.

Akane must have seen the expression on my face, and her eyes turned serious. "In my new position, I have some influence. I'll do everything I can to get you an audience." I looked at Akane and her gaze did not falter. The laughter had gone from her eyes and she seemed sincere in what she said.

"Thank you so much," I said, bowing enthusiastically. Finally there was a glimmer of action.

"Save your thanks for now," Akane said. "The Shogun is very busy and there are many people in line before you, awaiting an audience. I cannot guarantee when you will see him. But you *will* see him. You have my word."

I turned around to Mother and Hana. Their faces were shining with happiness. *Does Mother feel the need to apologize for me* now? I wondered. I waited for her thanks, but she lifted her cup and took another sip of tea.

Akane drank her tea and then placed her cup

down with finality. Our private audience with her had come to an end. Akane left through her door and the three of us went back out the door we came in, following a servant to a nearby hall where other women were filing in. Servants carried in the equipment and fresh flowers for *ikebana*.

"Aren't you glad I said something?" I whispered.

Mother inclined her head. "The outcome is good," she murmured. "Though I do wish the subject had been raised more . . . calmly." Before I could reply, she strode ahead into the room.

The Shogun's mother was waiting for us, seated on a raised platform. It was clear she wasn't here to arrange flowers, but to watch over the women and see how Akane performed in her new role.

We gathered quietly around the long tables that waited for us. I was startled by what I saw. Rows of twigs, flowers, blossoms, pots, and bamboo baskets. There were small cutting implements and bowls of moss. So much was needed for arranging flowers! With so many colors, shapes, and scents offered before me, I had no idea where to start. For a moment, I regretted that I had not paid more attention when Mother had supervised the flower arranging at home.

"I don't know what to do," I whispered to Hana as we kneeled beside a table. Hana reached over and picked out a long iris stem, topped by a violet-blue flower with a vivid yellow streak in its heart. She held it up to the light and turned it, scrutinizing the flower for imperfections. She seemed perfectly at ease and a gentle smile lit up her face.

"Just copy what I do," she whispered.

I stared at the flowers, feeling out of my depth. Akane came to kneel beside me, and panicking, I reached for a single lily. But its petals were brown at the tips and I could see that the stem had been crushed. I put it back down on the table.

Akane pulled a low container toward her and began to hold twigs and flowers above it, one by one, choosing an arrangement. As she worked, she quietly addressed me. "*Ikebana* traces the three points of life: heaven, earth, and man. If your arrangement can mimic this triangle, you have much to be proud of."

I noticed the way she arranged her flowers, and between their petals and the base of the container, I could see a triangle shape. It was so simple, and yet so clever.

The other women chatted as they worked on their simple arrangements. No flower was out of place, no blossom was allowed to overpower the whole arrangement. These privileged women were the heads of powerful clans, and flower arranging was almost as competitive as sword fighting. In bowls filled with moss, the women arranged their flowers in a graceful style that allowed each bloom to shine.

I backed away from the table, feeling frustrated. How was it that I could wield a sword with such confidence, yet I could not choose a single flower?

No one noticed as I extracted myself and kneeled near a wall, pressing my palms against its cool surface. No one, except the Shogun's mother, whose gaze flitted over me for just a moment—enough for me to know that she had seen me. Thankfully she didn't seem annoyed or shocked. But she saw everything, and in this way, she reminded me of Master Goku.

The room was filled with low murmurs as the women worked. Akane was busy admiring Hana's beautiful arrangement. My mother's head bowed over her work. Everyone was at peace—everyone except me. But at least now I had the chance to watch.

This must be what ninja feel like, I realized. Silent, unnoticed, watching. A couple of the women were casting glances in Mother's direction and smirking. One of them was the older woman who had been so rude yesterday. She cast a final, collusive glance at her friend and approached Mother.

She cleared her throat to draw Mother's attention. Mother glanced up from her arrangement and, for a moment, looked startled to see this woman again. But she quickly rearranged her features into a smile of polite welcome.

"I wondered," said the woman, speaking loudly so that everyone could hear. "Do you really think it's appropriate that a widow enjoys the privilege of the Administrator's hospitality? Surely, a woman without a husband has very little rank. What would you say?" The woman was clearly trying to challenge our family. Mother's smile never faltered and I had to admire her composure.

"Hospitality is open to all, I would have thought," Mother said quietly. "At least, the type of hospitality that is offered by a good and open heart." Mother waited for her words to find their aim. Anyone could see that, right now, this woman's heart was neither good nor open. The woman blushed and tried to straighten her crooked back. She picked up a stem of buds and went back to her arrangement. I looked at the Shogun's mother but found it impossible to read her face. She remained silent and allowed the women's conversation to continue.

A younger woman came to kneel beside Mother.

"I like your composition," she said, holding out a hand to brush the bamboo grass Mother had chosen. "It's very elegant." Mother smiled in acknowledgment and nodded at the younger woman's own arrangement.

"Camelias are so pretty at this time of year," she said, returning the kind words. A second woman came alongside, to inspect the arrangements. She looked at Mother's bamboo grass and sniffed.

"That doesn't last well at all," she said. "The tips will turn brown and faded in a day."

Mother cocked her head on one side, as if considering what the woman had said. "You may be right," she said diplomatically. "I must choose better next time."

The woman looked taken aback to see her criticism so well fielded. She looked around her, as if trying to find another target. At that moment, Hana reached out for a stem of sticky buds and the sleeve of her kimono caught on a twig. The red, angry scars from her burns were revealed for all to see, and the younger woman let out a gasp of sympathy.

"You poor thing!" she cried, reaching out to place a sympathetic hand on Hana's arm. Hana snatched her arm away and quickly rearranged the kimono, her face scarlet.

"It's nothing," she murmured.

"Such a shame," the second woman said. "It will be difficult to find a husband with those . . . imperfections."

Hana looked up, her eyes brimming with tears. She stod up from the table, abandoning her arrangement. I looked over at Akane, willing her to say something, but she was carrying her own *ikebana* over toward an alcove. Beyond her, the Shogun's mother nodded to a servant who helped her get to her feet. Then she walked out of the room. As she passed the woman who had last been talking, her lips narrowed. The woman had turned back to her flower arranging and did not notice. But I did.

"We must go now," I said, my voice trembling with anger. The Shogun's mother was not the only person who wanted to be away from this wasp hive. Mother did not try to protest as I led my sister from the room.

I slid open the door to our apartment and tore the wig off my head, throwing it on the floor. "Those women!" I said. Hana was openly crying now, and I shut the door so that no one could see into our room. "Don't let them see you cry. It would just make them happy." Hana's tears scored her cheeks and she threw herself onto her bed, hiding her face in the crook of her elbow. I tried to put a comforting hand on her shoulder, but she shrugged me off.

Mother stepped into the room. "They do not mean to hurt us," she said. But her eyes were also shiny with tears and she struggled to meet my gaze. My chest heaved as I struggled to contain my anger and frustration.

"Oh, they mean to hurt us," I said. I walked over to the window and gazed out at the blooming azalea.

How could a place so full of beauty also contain such hate? A wisp of fresh air encircled me and I suddenly ached to be outside. "We never should have come here."

"They will accept us eventually. They just need time," Mother said, sinking down to kneel on a mat. She put her head in her hands and suddenly looked exhausted. I glanced from her to Hana, who still wept.

"Look at what they've done to Hana. How dare they?" I walked to the door of the room and pushed it wide open. I wanted to get far away from those women and the luxurious rooms of the compound. I wanted to be back among people who had no time to be idle or indulge themselves with cruel words.

"What are you doing, Kimi?" Mother asked, looking up, her face worried.

"I'm going to give them a real scandal!" I said, striding out into the walkway.

CHAPTER EIGHTEEN

I tore down the walkways, pushing past the ladies in their kimonos. I barely registered where I was going, following the twists and turns until I plunged into a huge room at the rear of the compound. Clouds of steam filled the air and terse instructions were being shouted across the wide work surfaces. The kitchen! I thought again about my days working in the kitchen at Master Goku's, when my sister and I were in disguise as peasant serving boys. I remembered the sense of safety and security I felt as Choji set us to work. I strode forward and grabbed a knife from the table.

"Give me something to do," I said to the nearest person.

A girl the same height as me turned around and looked me up and down, taking in my fine robes. Her eyebrows arched in surprise. "Aren't you the daughter of . . ." She hesitated when she saw how angry I looked. "Are you lost?" she asked.

A man heaved a basket of vegetables onto the table. I grabbed a handful of spring onions and chopped them up finely. I could see that the servants didn't need my help—they doubtless wondered why the daughter of a noble was down here! But it helped my mood to be doing something other than arranging flowers or adjusting kimonos. All my kitchen training flooded back and I quickly raced through the stems of the onions with the sharp blade. It was instinctive and meditative, and as I worked, I felt the flush disappear from my cheeks and my heartbeat settle.

The girl shrugged and turned back to her own work. I glanced over at her and noticed that she must be about my age. She had a small, button nose and beautiful, high cheekbones. She cast a curious glance back at me.

"What's your name?" I asked, as I reached for a pile of ginger. I started to scrape the skin off with my knife, the pungent aroma filling my nose.

"Emiko," she said quietly and then hesitated. "What are you doing here? Aren't you one of the court families?"

I gave a hollow laugh. "I don't think the people up there think I'm courtly enough for them. I'm much happier here in the kitchens."

"But how . . . ?" I knew what Emiko wanted to ask. How did a girl of my breeding know how to handle a kitchen knife?

"It's a long story," I said.

Emiko gave a smile of understanding. "It's okay," she said. "I know all about secrets. I won't ask for any more details." I looked over at her and wondered what secrets she was talking about. Emiko waved the handle of her stubby kitchen knife at my head. "Your hair," she said. "It's . . ."

My hand raced to my temple and I realized that I had left my wig behind and the white streak was there for all to see. "I was in a fire, and my hair was burned off. When it grew back . . ." I shrugged my shoulders.

Emiko grinned. "It suits you," she said.

Then we both laughed and turned back to our work.

The time passed quickly. Too quickly. An older man approached us as Emiko and I scattered the last of the vegetable dressings over the platters. As I turned to greet him, I slipped the kitchen knife off the bench and hid it in the sleeve of my kimono. Who knew when it would come in useful? I should never have allowed myself to be persuaded to leave my sword behind at the monastery.

"Dinner is soon to be served," he said. "If you would like to return to the main hall, you may join your fellow diners." He didn't look directly at me but gazed over the top of my head.

191

I waited in silence until he eventually brought his glance down at my face. *He hates me for being here,* I thought. *He doesn't think it's right.* But I'd show him—I'd show everyone. If they wanted to use their rules to laugh at me, I would give them something to laugh about.

"I won't be dining tonight," I said, my voice firm. Servants strode past us, carrying huge platters of steamed rice and vegetables. One man staggered beneath a cauldron of miso soup.

"Won't your mother be asking for you?" the man-servant said quietly. His eyes beseeched me to do the "right" thing, the "proper" thing—to go back to my own quarters. I was breaking many codes of conduct being down here, and I could see that it made him uncomfortable. But I would not be moved.

Behind the man I could see a rough wooden table being loaded up with dishes made from the scraps of vegetables deemed too imperfect for the main hall. Steam rose off the food invitingly as the kitchen staff sat on the low benches and reached out with their chopsticks.

I nodded a head in their direction. "I'll be eating here tonight," I said.

Emiko let out a yip of excitement and raced over to the table. She kneeled and looked over at me, patting the empty space beside her on the floor.

"Excuse me," I said to the man as I went to walk past him. But he would not give way. I looked up at him and he continued to ignore me. Then I stepped to one side and walked around him.

The food was good. It was simple and filling, and that was all I needed. Chatter billowed up along with the clouds of steam, and Emiko and I laughed as we ate. Occasional thoughts of Mother, Hana, and Moriyasu bubbled into my head, but I quickly pushed them away. Would they be angry with me for abandoning them? For once, I did not care.

As the table was cleared, Emiko led me into a storeroom. "Can you sweep this out while I shift the bags of rice next door? It would win me a few extra moments of free time and I'd be so grateful." I looked at Emiko and wondered how much time she got to herself.

"Of course," I said, taking the broom from her. I worked around the room, determined to sweep up every last dot of dirt. It felt good to be using my body again.

When I was done, I walked through to the room next door to find Emiko. She was heaving something into a laundry basket. *What's a laundry basket doing in the kitchens?* I thought. I took a step closer and gasped. Emiko swirled around and stood clumsily in front of the basket, her face flushing red.

"What are you doing?" I asked.

Emiko took a step forward, trying to block my view. "Nothing!" she said with a false brightness.

I pushed past her.

"No!" she cried. But it was too late; I had already seen. A bag of rice sat underneath a crushed pile of linen. I turned back to my new friend. Behind her, the noise and clamor of the kitchen was starting up again as empty plates were brought back down from the main hall. People called out to one another as they rushed to clean up the kitchen. Out there were Emiko's friends. Did any of them know she was a thief? She could be put to death if the authorities found out.

"Why?" I asked quietly. Emiko's glance fell to her hands as her fingers twisted around themselves.

"It's for my family's village, past the protected village around the Shogun's compound," she said. She darted a desperate look at me. "The Shogun has more food than he knows what to do with. My family is starving! I know the Shogun doesn't realize how Lord Steward Yamamoto is punishing people with hunger, but I have to do something. There's food here to spare. How can I refuse to help my family?"

So this was what she meant by "secrets," I realized. I understood Emiko's reasons completely. "Do you work alone?" I asked.

Emiko shook her head. "There's a whole organization of us supplying villages in the estates of your uncle. My family would be dead of starvation by now, if it wasn't for the rice that is eked out of the Shogun's stores. But, Kimi, you mustn't tell anyone. Promise me?"

"I promise," I said. "And I'll do more than that— I'll help." I could try to put things right. "What can I do?"

Emiko smiled with relief. "Oh, thank you so much." She looked around the doorway of the room into the main kitchen. "I need to get the rice out through the laundry room and into the stables. But two of us will get the job done much quicker. We can carry a laundry basket each." She pulled a second basket off a shelf and shoved a bag of rice beneath a pile of bedsheets. Then she thrust the basket into my arms.

"Ready?" she asked. I nodded once. "Then let's go."

We left the kitchen by a side door that led into the laundry room. As we passed through, I noticed some of the other servants glance up at us—and then discreetly look away. *They know,* I thought. *They know what's happening and they're turning a blind eye.* I realized for the first time that the politics of the privileged were not so different from life in the kitchens. The compound was riddled with secrets in every corner.

The two of us walked through the heat of the

laundry room and emerged into the fresh air of the evening. The stables were nearby and we walked across the gravel, carrying our baskets. I prayed that no one would see us. Not only would our lives be in danger, but my family would surely never recover from the scandal. The gravel sounded noisily beneath our feet and I flinched when a stable door was suddenly thrown open, lamplight flooding over us. A man waved a hand and we scurried toward him, plunging into the stable just as he pulled the door shut behind us. As the stable door closed, I heard the voices of samurai soldiers outside on their rounds. A moment or two later, and Emiko and I would have been caught. We looked at each other, eyes wide, and let out nervous laughs.

"That was close," I said.

"Too close," said the man gruffly. "You must be quicker next time." Now I could see why Emiko needed help. Every day she was risking her life to help her people. It made my efforts to see the Shogun seem pathetic by comparison.

As we loaded the bags of rice into the man's saddlebags, Emiko and I chatted. It helped to dispel our nerves.

"We get to hear all the gossip as servants," she explained. "The lords and ladies don't have any discretion when we're around. Do you want to hear some secrets? Call it payment for your help!" Emiko lowered her voice even more. "Everyone's talking about which clans are going to set their allegiances over the land seizures—with the thunderous Kaminari or with the son of the respected *Jito*. Of course, all the people want to wait to see what the Administrator and Shogun decide. Your family is making big ripples." I had no idea so much had been going on behind the scenes.

"We hope that the Shogun will help us in our plight," I said. I decided to take a leap of faith and share my own secrets with my new friend. I told her what had really happened between our father and Uncle Hidehira, about our struggles and the battle to reinstate Moriyasu. I even told her about our vicious cousin Ken-ichi, son of our hated uncle, and how he had tormented us.

"What name did you say?" Emiko asked slowly.

"Ken-ichi," I said, frowning. "Why?" Emiko packed the last of the rice and buckled the saddle bag.

"I've heard that name," she said, thinking hard. "Yes! He came here to the compound, begging for entrance, not so long ago."

My heart beat loudly in my chest. "What happened?" I asked.

Emiko shrugged. "He was turned away. Never seen again." She opened the stable door a crack and peered outside. Then she turned and nodded sharply at me. "It's clear. Come on, we can run back to the kitchens." We waved a hand in farewell at the man who would take the rice to the starving villagers. Then we chased after each other across the gravel of the courtyard, falling through the kitchen doors one after the other.

"You'd better get back to your apartment now," Emiko said. "Thank you so much."

"Good-bye, Emiko," I said, as I turned to the walkway. "And good luck."

"And you," she called softly after me.

When I arrived back in my rooms, Mother was waiting for me, kneeling by the side of my bed. Moriyasu was deep in sleep, and Hana sighed and turned in her own bed. Mother's face was rigid and she called out no greeting. I walked stiffly over to my bed.

"How could you?" Mother asked, as she stroked a hand over my wig that she had rescued from the floor. "As if things weren't difficult enough for us, people were *outraged* by your absence at dinner. The servants told me you'd found your way to the kitchens. The kitchens!" I tried to take the wig from Mother, but she pulled it out of my grasp.

"You don't deserve this!" she said, her voice colder than I had ever heard before. "You don't deserve any of the things I've done to help you. Have you no shame?"

I kneeled down next to Mother. "I have shame," I replied. "I feel shame when I watch those people gorging on rich food. I feel shame when I see how ineffectual I've become. I feel shame when I watch my sister try to hide her scars and when you wince at my short hair. There's plenty of shame in my heart, Mother." When I finished, I felt a great sense of relief. But it did not change the fact that Mother thought what she wanted was the right thing.

She stood up and walked over to her own bed. As she undressed, she kept her back to me. She lay down in bed and gave me one final look. "You behave like a petulant child, Kimi. When will you learn?" She extinguished her light and the room was plunged into darkness.

I was left to undress blindly. As I laid down on the floor, I could hear Hana sobbing quietly. *I've gone too far*, I thought. *I must learn to control my anger.* Unhappily I turned over and tried to sleep, though I doubted it would come easily.

CHAPTER NINETEEN

As the days passed, I worked with a new resolve to fit in with the nobility by which I was surrounded. I joined Hana as she recited poetry, I worked hard at my flower arranging, and I even joined the women as they embroidered *temari* balls for the children, my fingers bleeding and sore from the pricks of the needle in my clumsy hands. Slowly Mother began to forgive me. But I had to work hard to retrieve her affection. Thank goodness Moriyasu was much quicker to forget—he challenged me to daily games of Go and we both kept improving. Hana flitted about the court, charming the men and women like a songbird. We got occasional glimpses of Tatsuya, as he guarded the compound, but we didn't have another chance to speak to him in private and he refused to meet our glance as he marched past.

I wondered what was going on outside the compound. Emiko would pause by our rooms sometimes, on her way to the kitchen, and give me details of the estates. She even shared more secrets from court.

"The latest gossip is that your family's cause is gaining ground. People feel sorry for you and all the clans are waiting to hear what the Shogun will say," she told me one morning.

I gave a hollow laugh. "If pity helps my family win, I'll take it all!" I joked. There was only one question that still plagued me, circling my mind. What was Uncle planning? There had been little word of him and I did not trust this silence.

One evening, as the mists gathered in the courtyard, Akane stopped by our apartment. It was rare to see her outside of the Administrator's rooms and we scrambled to our feet to greet her.

"Good evening," Mother said, bowing low.

Akane was dressed in a primrose-blue kimono with a red obi sash. She glanced around the room and her nose crinkled. Mother threw Hana and me an alarmed glance.

"These rooms are so cramped," Akane said, ducking her head to walk through the doorway, though it was more than tall enough to accommodate her height. "You must have new rooms immediately!"

Mother blinked in confusion. "We are very happy here. The Shogun has been most kind."

She shook her head vehemently. "No," she decided. She walked quickly out onto the walkway and signaled to a servant. She pointed into the room. "Pack up their belongings immediately. This family is moving to my apartments."

The servant cast us an impressed glance and began picking up our personal belongings. My hand twitched to snatch my clothes out of her hands—I wanted to organize my own things! But I knew I could not afford to offend Akane. We watched as servants rifled through our belongings. Then Akane waved a hand at the doorway.

"Follow me," she said. Her actions were meant to be kind, but I had the feeling we were being issued a command that would brook no contest. Hana smiled weakly at me and we followed her out of the room.

When we arrived in Akane's wing of the compound, more servants jumped to attention. We were shown into a set of rooms that were beautiful by merit of their simplicity. Everything here made our previous apartment seem gaudy: The tatami mats were clean and aromatic, the paper screens discreet. In one room was a folding screen decorated with pheasants and peonies; in another stood a single, perfect orchid in the alcove. As we walked from room to room, gazing around us, we realized that Akane had given us a room each. Moriyasu's room was decorated with replicas of samurai equipment and implements. He ran into the room and shouted out in delight.

Mother turned to our hostess and smiled. "But why?" she asked. "We were perfectly happy where we were."

"I wasn't," Akane said, as servants unrolled the mattresses. "I had to go down endless walkways if I wanted to see you." Hana and I shared a glance—this was the first time Akane had ever tried to visit us. "I want good people by my side. Please, make yourselves comfortable."

Hana kneeled in front of one of the scrolls that hung on a wall. It carried an elegant poem and I could see her trying to memorize it. Mother was unpacking our things and handed over my Go board.

"Go! You play?" Akane asked and when I nodded, a competitive smile broke out on her face. "I would be honored if you shared a game with me."

I was happy for the challenge and wondered what type of player Akane would be. I sat on one side of a low table, and Akane kneeled on the other. We both gazed at the squares scored on the board, and I waited to see where Akane would place her first pebble. She lifted it between her forefinger and middle finger and her hand hovered above the board. Then she brought the pebble down with a sharp click.

She had placed it slightly off center, with no clear indication of her plan and she continued by spreading her black, shiny stones in different places on the board. There was no single allegiance here, no loyal grouping of pebbles. I was confused and increasingly uncertain of my own moves. I tried to bring my pebbles close to Akane's, so that I was ready to capture. I'd used this technique to capture many of my brother's pebbles, but Akane ignored my tactic and continued to calmly arrange different groups of pebbles across the board. I became uncertain—which group should I try to surround? I changed my tactics and—too late—realized my mistake. Within a few easy moves, Akane had closed in like a net around a group of my small white pebbles. I was surrounded.

"You're losing, Kimi," she said, her cheeks flushed red with excitement. I studied the board and realized that Akane had been a politician. She had been spreading herself thinly—it was true—but she had covered all her options. Akane had followed one of the golden rules of Go that Daisuke had shared with me: "The only person who can make you lose is you," Daisuke had said. "You need to see into yourself, understand your own moves, to win." I looked at Akane. Clearly she had no intention of allowing herself to lose; she had looked deep into her own soul and found the strength to conquer. Could I ever be as determined?

I nodded my head in congratulations and was about to suggest another game when my opponent got to her feet. A cool breeze came in through an open window and I realized that the night was turning cold.

"I must retire now," she said. She nodded at the board. "It's all about territory and influence. Find the balance and the board is yours."

Before I could thank her, Akane was already walking to the door. With a regal wave of her hand, she departed. I looked at Mother and Hana and they were both watching the empty space Akane had left behind her, surprised expressions on their faces.

"Time for bed," Mother said sharply. "Come on, all of you."

"Another new bed! How many have I slept in these past weeks?" Moriyasu joked, as he ran to his room. I dragged my covers off the bed and wrapped myself up as I lay on the cool floorboards.

"Why do you think Lady Akane has brought us to these rooms?" Hana asked.

"I don't know. Enough talk," Mother said. "It gets in the way of sleeping."

Mother retired and Hana climbed beneath her bed covers. There was a fourth room for Hana, but we did not want to be parted—not even for a night—so we had dragged her mattress through to my room. I listened to the sounds from outside—the cooing of the birds as they settled for the night, and the branches of the trees shifting in the breeze. I listened for other noises, too—for the snap of a twig or the telltale crunch of gravel—but everything was quiet. We would be safe here, so close to the Shogun.

I turned over and waited for the kiss of sleep. It did not arrive. I looked over my shoulder and saw Hana padding to a window where she pulled back the screen. Above us, stars twinkled in the night sky. I thought of the head scarf—midnight blue with pinpricks of white—that Daisuke asked for. *What is he doing now?* I wondered, not for the first time.

"Kimi!" Hana whispered, interrupting my thoughts. I sat up sharply in bed and looked over at her. She pointed out of the window at something, and I scrambled out of bed to sit beside her at the open window. She squeezed my arm and pointed again.

It was a night heron. It must be after the water in the pool. I could just make out the patches of blue around its eyes, and the bird's tawny red feathers reflected the glitter of the pond water. It was beautiful.

When I looked back at Hana, she was watching my face.

"What?" I asked. Hana gazed back out of the window. The heron spread its wings and flew over the walls of the compound.

"Why did you go to the kitchen?" she asked, as

we watched the bird soar into the sky. "Why did you want to make things difficult for us?"

I stayed silent for a moment, still watching the heron. I wished that I could follow it . . . be free . . . free to do all the things I needed to. "I just want to see things *happen*, Hana," I finally said. "After all we have been through, we're reduced to dressing up like ladies and bowing our heads, keeping quiet and arranging flowers. How is this helping the estates?"

Hana opened her mouth to speak when—

"What's that?" I whispered, holding up a hand to silence my sister. Beneath the wings of the heron I had noticed a flicker of light down on the ground— the white of an eye.

"What?" Hana started to ask, but I jerked my head at a corner of the courtyard. Hana's eyes widened as she saw what I had already noticed.

The figure of a man. A ninja!

He was dressed all in brown with a cowl wrapped around his head. He pressed himself against the wall of the compound as he followed its contours around the courtyard, moving away from the Shogun's rooms—toward an almost unnoticeable rope hanging over the wall high off the ground.

"Has he attacked the Shogun? Oh no!" Hana whispered. We watched as the person leaped up into the branches of a tree and then reached out for the rope. He leaned dangerously far out and caught hold of the rope, dragging it through the air toward him. He pulled it tight. After a final glance behind him, he threw himself forward so that the soles of his feet braced against the taut rope and his hands held him steady. Then he climbed. He was *walking* up the wall!

I jumped to my feet. "Come on, Hana! We can't let him get away!" We raced out of the room—a side door took us directly out to the garden. Hana moved to run across the gravel, but I pulled her back. The crunch of those pebbles would surely give us away. I pointed toward the compound's wall.

"If we can get over there, we can climb the wall and follow the ninja." The main building was bordered by swept sand, soft and silent underfoot. We crept forward until we were against the wall. I felt for fingerholds between the stones and climbed. I could hear Hana giving small grunts of exertion as she followed.

Quickly I scaled the wall, pain searing my hands and feet as I crammed them between the hard edges of the stones. The mist had come down thick now, and it was difficult to see where the anonymous figure had gone—but I could just make him out feeling his way across the top of the wall, moving farther into the compound. I had thought he had been making his escape—I was wrong. *He's using the wall to walk over the top of our heads,* I thought. It was a clever plan to move around without being seen. But where was he going?

I reached the top of the wall and heaved Hana up beside me. She was panting—having lost some quickness and stamina during her recovery. I pointed to where we could barely see the intruder balancing on top of the wall. Fortunately the compound wall was made of thick stones and we could hurry, holding our arms out for balance. Just as we were about to catch up with the faceless man, he jumped down from the wall and landed with a small thud beside three others inside the compound. We had stumbled upon a secret ninja meeting. But how could we get close enough to hear what they were saying?

As they talked, the men walked along the base of the wall. I waited until they had gone a safe distance and then dropped down into the soft soil at the roots of a yew bush. The dense leaves were just enough to keep me hidden. I looked up at Hana and smiled to let her know I was fine; she smiled back and pulled her head out of sight. Then I waited, trying to keep my breathing quiet.

The men paused, heads close together as they talked. I could see the man we'd first followed speaking animatedly. One of the men shook his head vehemently, then all four of them turned and walked back toward me. Soon they came close enough so that I could hear what they were saying.

"Wait for orders," one of them said in a low voice. The figure in brown hesitated, then nodded. "Succeed in your mission, and you'll get your heart's desire. Fail . . ." That last word hung in the air with dreadful weight. "And you will be bound to us forever." I shuddered and the man nodded again in understanding.

Then the four men walked away to a smoother section of the wall. Three of them scaled it, with the mysterious man in brown watching. They didn't use a rope. One of them flung up what looked like a collapsible bamboo pole. Its hook caught the top of the wall and the man started to climb. Another used two hand knives to climb, piercing between the stones of the wall to find a sticking place for the blades to heave himself up. The third followed the first up the bamboo pole. I looked up and motioned to Hana to join me. She fell through the air and landed beside me, allowing herself to fall to her knees to soften the impact and then quickly standing up again.

The man dressed in brown turned away and followed the line of the wall back to the rooms of the compound. Something about his manner seemed less tense now—as if he was retiring.

That's it! I thought. *He lives here.*

"He's one of us," Hana said breathlessly. "He must live on the Shogun's compound." But as we watched the man walk away, he seemed to disappear into the night. I swung around, looking for clues. Where had he gone?

"We've lost him!" I said.

"No. Come on. Let's track him down," Hana replied, picking up speed. The two of us picked our way around the courtyard, peering into bushes and watching for reflections in the ponds' still waters. As I gazed down into the smooth surface of the largest pond, I saw a shadow pass behind my head.

"Hana—"

A foot landed in the small of my back, pushing me forward so that my head plunged into the ice-cold water. I rolled onto my back and kicked my feet into the air, propelling myself up into a standing position. I gave a double-handed punch and felt the taut skin of a stomach beneath my fist. The man gasped in pain. My eyes adjusted to the night, and I could see him writhing on the ground. I brought my foot up and prepared to smash my heel into his face, but then I changed my mind and arced my leg around in a low kick that caught his cowl and tore it from his head.

"Who are you?" I hissed, lunging forward, trying

to see what my attack had revealed. But whoever he was scrambled away and pulled the fabric over his face, before springing back up. He kicked out his right heel, straight into my shoulder. The impact sent me spinning and I fell to my knees but I caught a glimpse of skin in the moonlight. Across its surface was the black ink of a tattoo—the distinctive *kanji* tattoo of the brotherhood of ninja.

The side of his hand came down on the back of my neck and I fought against the dizziness, heaving myself to my hands and knees just in time to see the brown-clad figure racing away. He plunged into the compound. Our enemy had escaped. Somewhere, in there, he was hidden.

Hana raced to my side. I could see a trickle of blood, black as tar in the darkness, on her right leg. She helped me to my feet.

"He kicked me," she explained. "But I'm fine." As she helped me across the courtyard, we heard the unmistakable sound of marching feet. The Shogun's samurai soldiers! We could not be caught out of our rooms.

"Come on, Hana! Quickly!" I said, gripping my side as I heaved myself back to our apartment's side door. We tumbled through the door, lungs scorching from our exertions. I caught my breath and opened the main door of our room, to make sure no one had noticed our absence. A slither of moonlight flooded ahead of me, lighting up the profile of a woman. It was Akane, pushing open the door to Moriyasu's room.

"What's going on?" I asked, as she froze in the moonlight. She looked back at me in surprise.

She straightened up and pulled her robes tighter around her body. She shook her head, smiling, and closed the door again. "I thought I heard noises," she explained.

It made my heart leap. Had the ninja come back here, to Moriyasu's room? I did not dare ask more; did not want to reveal that I had been away.

Hana came up behind me. "What is it? What's wrong?" she asked. I looked around.

"Go back to bed," Akane whispered. "It must have been nothing." Then she glided across the floor and was gone.

I turned back to Hana. What if it wasn't nothing? What if Uncle was sending ninja even into the house of the Shogun to assassinate our brother? The two of us looked at each other, frightened. Too much had happened tonight. I walked past Hana and lay down on my bed. As she stood in the doorway, watching me, Hana looked suddenly very tired.

"Go to bed," I said. "We'll talk tomorrow. But . . ." My sister looked at me questioningly. "From now on,

I will sleep with my weapon beside me." I reached into one of my bags in the corner of the room and retrieved the knife that I had stolen from the kitchen. I held it up, and its scratched blade caught the moonlight. Hana gasped, and I put it under my pillow, ready to be used.

CHAPTER TWENTY

The next day was close and muggy. I had barely slept; the image of our faceless enemy in the compound twisted through my troubled thoughts. Who could it be? I would be extra vigilant—inspect every face and keep an eye out for unusual behavior. This man would give himself away sooner or later—and when he did I would be ready.

That morning, we had been invited by Akane to stroll the grounds of the compound with her.

As we stepped outside, Akane bent her head in greeting. Behind her was the Administrator and an entourage of other noble women. We walked from the courtyard to the pond garden and then over to where vegetables and herbs were grown. Akane was knowledgeable and pointed out some of the more unusual herbs. I felt a stab of longing for my friend Daisuke—I preferred his lessons.

The compound was alive with activity. Horses

stood outside of their stables, being groomed, while the kitchen staff kneeled in the dirt, digging vegetables for that day's meals. I could see Emiko among them, and as she wiped the back of her hand across her brow, she grinned at me. It was the most communication we could dare to share in a public place like this. Samurai soldiers circuited the compound.

As we walked, I watched. I drew close to passers-by and tried to see the skin of their throats, servants and samurai alike. Where was that tattoo I had seen so distinctly last night? People paused in their activities to greet the Administrator and his wife, and as we patiently waited for the pleasantries to end, I would narrow my eyes and wait for a giveaway turn of the head.

"What are you doing?" Hana asked, drawing up beside me.

"Looking for that tattoo," I whispered. I had told her about it last night, as we lay in bed. I heard Hana tut.

"Leave it, Kimi," she said. "We risked our lives last night—for nothing. We should forget the whole thing. An audience with the Shogun will serve us much better."

Now it was my turn to feel frustrated. "What are you talking about?" I asked. "Can't you see? We've been here for days and achieved barely anything. After last night, we can't just leave it. That enemy is *here*—laughing in our faces. He could be after Moriyasu."

Hana shook her head. As I watched her walk away from me, I realized my sister and I wanted totally different things.

I looked around me. A samurai strode past and I stood on my tiptoes, craning to see past his high, iron-paneled collar. He stared back at me and I quickly turned away. Nothing. I bit my lip as I tried to think. *How can I find out who the tattoo belongs to? Who knows everything and everyone in this compound?* Emiko! That was it! I could ask her to help me in my search.

A clap of thunder rang out and women cried out in shock. *Fools!* I thought as people scurried indoors, scared of a bit of rain. I would have stayed, but Hana grabbed my hand and pulled me after her. We plunged into a walkway and followed the court people back to our rooms. As we turned a corner, we stumbled into an armored soldier who was standing guard in the walkway. He turned fiercely—it was Tatsuya.

Hana and I allowed the rest of the court to pull ahead; we could catch up with them later.

"Forgive us," Hana hurriedly apologized. "We were escaping the thunderstorm." Tatsuya's eyes softened and I glimpsed a moment of affection for my sister. She saw it, too, and took a hesitant step closer. We had not had a chance to speak to Tatsuya since our meeting in the pond garden.

"I am so proud of you," Hana whispered.

Tatsuya's face flooded with pleasure.

"Yes," I said. "You look so handsome in your samurai uniform—like a real warrior. Did your time with the ninjas teach you any special tricks?" Tatsuya's smile melted away at the sound of my voice.

"Please, Tatsuya," Hana wheedled. She could see that his mood had turned black. "We're your friends, remember." He stepped backward, creating a space between us.

"Noble girls should not speak to samurai so . . . casually," he said, his voice cold and formal. "Please, do not compromise me this way." His glance flickered over toward me and I saw his lip curl. "Besides . . . I do not wish to associate with girls who leave the court for kitchen life. Such lack of decorum."

I felt as though I had been slapped in the face. Tatsuya, of all people, should understand. He had earned our friendship by risking his life for us, and now his actions told us that we meant nothing to him anymore.

Hana turned away to hide her face. I could see her shoulders shake and I knew that tears would be streaking her cheeks.

"How could you?" I asked Tatsuya.

A moment's guilt showed in his face, and as he looked at Hana, I could see his resolve flounder. He took a step toward her, but an order rang out from a hidden part of the samurai's quarters and he turned on his heel, marching away. He did not look back.

Hana wheeled around. Her face was red and distorted. In her anger, her kimono sleeves had slipped back and I could see her tender scars.

"This is your fault!" she cried. "All of it!" A woman scurried past and stared at us, scandalized at the raised voices. Hana no longer cared. "If you hadn't offended Tatsuya, he would still be our friend." Her voice broke. "Now we are friendless and you seem intent on ruining our chances at court. For all of our sakes, Kimi, leave things be. Allow us a *chance!*" She pushed past me toward our room, but a voice called out from behind us. We both turned around to see Mother running toward us.

"Girls," she said. "I've been looking for you. It's happened." I gazed from Mother to Hana and back again. Hana rubbed her knuckles across her face to dry the tears.

Moriyasu pushed past Mother's skirts to stand before me in the walkway. "Mother did it!" he said.

"She's gotten us an audience with the Shogun!"

I looked at Mother, stunned. "How?" I asked.

"It's all due to Lady Akane," said Mother. "She was called to see the Shogun. When she came back she said she'd asked for an audience on our behalf—and he said yes!" She turned back down the walkway, toward the main hall. "Come *on*, Kimi!" she said over her shoulder, her face flushed.

As I followed my family toward the hall, I could think only one thing. *Why now? Why all of a sudden?* Things were moving quickly. Too quickly. Akane had told us that it might take weeks to have our audience with the Shogun—and suddenly she had managed to set wheels in motion in a day? And I couldn't help remembering what Mother said: that if we failed, we could be banished. We would have to be very careful in this meeting.

As a second clap of thunder sounded, we were ushered into the Shogun's meeting room. The aggressive beat of heavy rain struck the roof above our heads. The Shogun's private rooms were away from the main hall. He kneeled on a scarlet rug, shoulders erect and hair oiled back. Behind him was a painted wall panel, depicting the flight of herons. On either side of him stood rows of samurai soldiers. I spotted Tatsuya, his face like ice.

To the Shogun's side sat his mother. She watched

as we kneeled and bowed low in front of the Shogun. When I straightened up, she was no longer looking at us. Her gaze rose above our heads, steady and impervious. She was like a statue, hewed from marble.

The Shogun indicated with a hand. "My mother attends all my meetings," he explained. "I am almost as wise as she is, but not quite." I saw a flicker of amusement pass over his face and knew I was allowed to smile—but the older woman's face remained impassive.

The Shogun nodded to a servant, who scurried over and kneeled before him. The Shogun spoke quietly to him, then the man turned to face us. "The Shogun wishes to hear your case," he announced.

My mother straightened her back even more and spoke. She told the Shogun about Uncle's attack on our family, about the murder of our father. She spared no details. It must have been a trial for my mother, to relive that day, but her voice never faltered and her hands were steady as she drew pictures with her words. There was still tension between Hana and me, but we stood together in support of Mother's plea.

"Lord Steward Yamamoto no Hidehira will never be satisfied," she said, drawing to a conclusion. "His thirst for power is unquenchable." She paused to let her meaning sink in. "Unless . . ." She looked at the

Shogun, the light of hope flooding her face. "Unless you will bring your forces against him. If you do, thousands of lives will be saved. If you don't, I dare not think . . ."

My pulse quickened. This speech of Mother's was a risky strategy. She was in danger of calling the Shogun a murderer—telling him he would be responsible for the loss of innocent lives if he did nothing. Mother and the Shogun gazed at each other for long moments. Then I noticed the older woman nod her head. The Shogun turned his face, noticing, too. Finally he addressed us directly.

"Your husband was a great man," he said. He looked over at Moriyasu, who kneeled patiently next to Hana. "And your son has impressed everyone during his stay here. I am sure he will be a great man, too." Moriyasu's face split in a wide smile, and I felt relief that he did not want to banish us. Then the Shogun's face turned serious. "But I do not think fighting is the solution. I could persuade Hidehira to divide the estates—it will appeal to his ego and still allow Moriyasu to have what is his by right."

More words! I thought. *Why is no one willing to take action?*

Mother shook her head. "I am so sorry. But I know my brother-in-law will never agree to that. He has already stolen so much territory and his appetite is not sated. He wants everything. Won't you recon-sider?"

Before the Shogun could reply, a door was flung open. Samurai soldiers jumped to their feet and raised their swords, ready to defend.

But when a cowering messenger appeared, the Shogun called out, "Stand down!"

The soldiers, including Tatsuya, sheathed their swords again. The messenger walked swiftly across the room, glancing nervously at the men in their pan-eled armor. He kneeled and held out a scroll to the Shogun, who took the paper, reading quickly. Then he glanced over at his mother.

"A small envoy of Zen monks," he said. "They want an audience immediately."

The Shogun's mother raised her eyebrows in surprise. "Their visits are rare," she said. Her voice sounded resonantly, like well-oiled mahogany. "It must be important."

"Bring them in," the Shogun said. He waved a hand at Mother and she climbed to her feet, indicat-ing to the rest of us that we should get out of the way. We scurried to the side of the room as five monks marched in. I was frustrated; our visit had been cut short and we had not reached the outcome I was counting on.

Rainwater poured down the monks. I could see

their *kote* armored sleeves beneath their robes and each carried a vicious-looking *naginata* staff with a curved blade. From their waists hung *katanas*, worn with the blade facing down. Some also carried *tanto* daggers.

Bringing such weaponry in front of the Shogun was almost unheard of. I felt the hairs stiffen on the back of my neck. The Shogun remained calm, and respect shone in his eyes.

A monk stepped forward. I had to bite my lip to prevent myself from crying out with joy. It was Daisuke! He looked different in his armor—not like the gentle monk whose hands had tended to my sister and me. His face shone as he kneeled before the Shogun.

"Master Satoshi has asked me to bring you this message: The Lord Steward Yamamoto no Hidehira has encroached on the land of our monastery," Daisuke said. "He is slowly surrounding us. Soon, he will attack. We ask your help."

The Shogun looked taken aback.

"We will not surrender, but the army he has sent outnumber us four to one," Daisuke went on. My heart sank. That was what Uncle had been up to in those quiet days: gathering men and targeting more land for capture. "Please send us some samurai and give your blessing for us to attack him first."

The Shogun hesitated and I could stand by no longer.

The words Daisuke had spoken to me just before I left the monastery echoed in my mind. I would have to use words as my weapons here. "He won't stop there," I blurted out. "He will take the monastery and will build his armies until he has enough strength to take on anyone. I think he aims for the highest prize—the title of Shogun."

Mother gasped at my boldness, as tension grew in the room.

The Shogun got to his feet—in anger at my temerity? My nails dug into the palms of my hands. I could hear Hana's breathing beside me, fast and shallow. Mother had put an arm around Moriyasu's shoulders. How would the Shogun respond?

The Shogun glanced once at his mother. She had not moved. Then he stepped down from the raised platform and approached Daisuke.

"With my blessing, you inhabit your monastery and lands," the Shogun said quietly. "It is a shame that Hidehira seems to feel free to . . . encroach on our neighborliness. He is pushing himself into places where he is not welcome."

It seemed the Shogun was taking my strong words seriously. The monks shifted on their knees and murmured among themselves. Beyond them, I could see a square of light through an open window. The clouds were clearing and the heavy rain was melting away.

The Shogun turned to face the main doors of the room.

"Bring the Administrator here. Immediately!"

CHAPTER TWENTY-ONE

A servant nodded once and hurried out of the room.

"I had no idea that a cuckoo was in the nest," the Shogun admitted, looking over to me. He regarded me for a moment and then turned back to Daisuke. "I have tolerated the Lord Steward's campaigns for power until now, but no more." His brow furrowed and he brought his hands together, raising his fingertips to his lips as he thought.

"What will you do?" Daisuke asked gently. "We need to know."

The Shogun looked past Daisuke to his mother, who still sat on the raised platform. I watched her closely and noted the way that she gazed back at her son. Her face didn't change, but I saw her hand move toward her obi sash and for the first time I realized that this woman had a dagger by her side. Her hand came to rest on its hilt, as if ready for action. Was she telling her son something?

"I will call a meeting," the Shogun decided. His mother's grip tightened around the dagger. "With the councillors. The heads of the clans will decide with me what should be done. If I'm to take action, I need good advice first."

The doors to the room were flung open and the Administrator stepped inside. His face was smooth and unlined, but I could see that his smile was forced.

"You called for me?" he asked, kneeling.

"Yes," the Shogun snapped. He strode across the room. "Why have we not been informed of the aggressive campaign of Lord Hidehira? Why have you not told us about his latest attacks? Are we to be kept blind to the suffering of our people?"

The Administrator shifted nervously, as the Shogun's mother looked on. "I apologize if I have offended you," he said. "I thought matters were under control. I did not want to worry you with trivial details."

"There is nothing trivial here. The monks are under attack!" The Shogun flung an arm out at Daisuke and his fellow warriors. "Your men must have known this. When were you going to tell us?"

The atmosphere in the room was tense. I could not bear to look at the man who had allowed our friends, the monks, to fight alone. I noticed that Hana's gaze

228

had fallen to the floor also. Long moments passed.

"Go," the Shogun eventually said, walking back to his place on the raised platform. "Leave us." He turned to address the room. "All lords should be in attendance tomorrow. We will have a formal discussion of recent—and future—events." People turned to the door of the room and filed out. Mother nodded to us, and we followed. I looked one last time at the Shogun's mother. Our eyes met and she smiled.

As I turned back, I saw the Administrator bow low to her, but the smile quickly faded from his face. I could only guess that she had not acknowledged his bow. He backed out of the room, beside us.

Out in the main hall, I hurried over to Daisuke.

"It's so good to see you!" I said, but Moriyasu pushed in front of me.

"I beat Kimi at three games of Go in a row!" he said proudly.

Daisuke laughed and looked over at me. "Is this true, Kimi? You may need your strategies more than ever now." Daisuke looked out of a window at the garden. "Can we talk outside?" he said. "There is much for us to speak of."

Behind Daisuke, I could see Hana waiting with Mother, who had a worried look on her face. I shook my head. "Can we meet later?" I asked. "My family needs me now. We were in the middle of a meeting

229

with the Shogun when you arrived."

Daisuke bowed. "I understand. Things are moving quickly. We will speak later." I watched him join the rest of the warrior monks, who were waiting farther down the walkway, then hurried to my mother and sister.

"We need to talk," Mother whispered to Hana, Moriyasu, and me. "Quickly back to our rooms!"

We walked back to our quarters and Mother pulled the sliding door shut behind her. Then she turned to face us, her cheeks flushed pink.

"This is the best chance we've ever had against your uncle," she said, coming to sit on the bed beside Hana. Moriyasu listened hard from his position in a corner of the room. "We have put our case to the Shogun and so have the monks. Two sets of people driving home the message that Uncle is a serious threat. We are lucky indeed that Daisuke arrived when he did. Together, we may well persuade the Shogun to take up arms."

I could hear the blood pounding in my ears. Finally, after all this time, was I to be handed the chance to fight for justice?

"In the next few hours, I need you all to stay strong and support one another in whatever comes next," Mother said, looking at us carefully. I wondered if she could sense the tension between Hana and me.

230

Moriyasu nodded his head vigorously. "Of course!" he told us, striding into the center of the room.

I smiled to myself; my little brother was growing up. I glanced at Hana, who looked back at me as if to say that she would tolerate me for the next few hours.

Mother held up a hand. "We will need to keep our nerve. If the Shogun picks up on any uncertainty or fear, it could be our undoing. We have to show that we are worthy. We must wear brave faces. Can you promise me to try?"

I kneeled before Hana and my mother. Moriyasu came beside me.

"Yes, Mother," I said. "I promise."

Not long after, Moriyasu, Hana, and I met Daisuke at one of the benches in the pond garden.

"What has happened since we last saw you?" I asked. A petal from the azalea floated down through the air and came to rest in Daisuke's lap. He lifted it and smelled its aroma before casting it to float across the water of the pond.

"We had to evacuate the infirmary," he began. "We did not want the sick and elderly suffering in an attack." His lips drew tight and I could see that painful memories were playing out in his head.

"Tell us," Hana said softly.

"Not everyone was strong enough for the trip." Moriyasu gazed up at Daisuke and I could see his lip tremble.

Moriyasu shook his head. "No," he said, pulling away across the bench. "Please tell me it's not true." I guessed my brother was thinking about the little girl and boy he had said good-bye to at the gates of the monastery.

"Don't worry," Daisuke said. "Your friends were among the lucky ones. They survived the journey. But others didn't."

Our brother got to his feet. He looked over at Hana and me. "I must go and tell Mother," he said. We watched Moriyasu walk away from us, back to our rooms.

"He will make a good leader," Daisuke said.

Daisuke reached a hand into a bag that he had been carrying. I recognized this bag—it was the one he had taken on our trip collecting herbs. He pulled out a ceramic jar.

"Hana's medicine!" I cried out in delight. Memories of collecting the sunflower seeds flooded back, and in my imagination I felt the heat of the sun once again. Daisuke passed the jar to Hana.

"Mother will be able to rub this in for me," she said, getting to her feet. Then she bowed to Daisuke and hurried away. I didn't mind that Hana had left us alone; I wanted to tell him about the man we had followed.

"There's a ninja here, in the grounds of the compound," I said in a low voice.

"Where?" he asked, looking around him.

"I don't know. Hana and I saw a man creep out one night to meet three ninja who had scaled the wall. He attacked us and I caught sight of his tattoo." I described the strokes scored across the man's skin.

Daisuke nodded. "The same sign we saw when the monastery was attacked," he said. "I've been asking some discreet questions. The villagers tell me that's the sign of the most powerful ninja family of all."

"Well, whoever he is, he's still here somewhere," I said. "He disappeared into the walkways, and we lost him. But he's definitely in the compound. What are we going to do? Hana doesn't want to get involved anymore, but I don't see how we can let this go. There's a killer in our midst!"

Daisuke gotten to his feet. "You're right. First, we will speak to your sister. She needs to understand how serious this is." Daisuke strode across the courtyard, and I ran to keep up. I led him to our rooms, but Hana was nowhere to be found. Moriyasu was practicing Go, alone.

"She went out to the Administrator's garden," he said, without looking up. "Mother's busy, so Hana went to sit outside with her oil."

I had never stepped foot into this part of the Administrator's garden before—at least, not during daylight hours. Hana must have been given an invitation to sit there by Akane.

We found Hana sitting beneath a maple tree. She smiled to herself as she rubbed the glistening oil across her arm. "Look!" she greeted us. We gazed at her scars and could see the skin glisten a healthy pink. The oil was saturating her skin with goodness; it could only be a matter of time before the scars faded completely.

Hana turned her arms in the sunshine. They looked like the necks of swans, as she circled her limbs gracefully through the air. She gazed up at us, delighted, and Daisuke smiled back at her. Then Hana's face froze.

"What is it?" I asked. She looked past me and her hands fell to her lap as she hurried to cover her arms again. She scrambled to her feet, almost knocking over the precious jar of oil.

"Let me explain . . . ," she started to say. I swiveled around and saw Tatsuya.

He stood, frozen on the spot, staring at the scars on Hana's arms. He twisted away, as though trying to deny what he had just seen.

"I was in a fire," Hana said. "I was trying to rescue

Kimi . . ." Her sentence trailed off. Tatsuya was backing away, shaking his head slowly. I could see that he didn't want to know, didn't want to hear what had happened to us without him by our side.

"I am on guard duty," he stuttered. "I cannot stop to talk." He looked up, once, at Hana's beautiful face.

Her eyes were brimming with tears. "Don't, Tatsuya," she begged him, her voice breaking. But he turned on his heel and marched away, pushing past a couple of samurai soldiers coming the other way.

"Fool!" one of them called after him. "Show more respect."

I couldn't have put it better myself. I turned back to my sister and tried to touch my fingertips to her own, in our secret signal of kinship. I wanted to comfort her. She pushed me away angrily.

The look in my sister's eyes at that moment was one I had never seen before. Disgust. And it was aimed at me.

"This is your fault," she said. "If you hadn't jumped out from our hiding place back in the innkeeper's hut, none of this would ever have happened to me." She raised her arm and shook it in my face.

"Please, Hana. Don't," I pleaded.

"Don't what? Tell you the truth?" With her kimono billowing behind her, she ran out of the garden.

I took a step to follow her.

"No, Kimi," Daisuke said. I had almost forgotten he was there. "Leave her be. She needs time. She will apologize for what she's said today."

I looked at the empty space where my sister had been only a few moments before. Was I the person who had made Hana this angry? I shook my head and brought my hands up to cover my face. *Did I really do this to my sister?* I thought.

I heard the crunch of gravel as Daisuke came to stand beside me.

"Time heals all wounds, my master tells me," he said. "Even wounds to the heart. Your sister is angry now, but she won't be forever. In the meantime, be patient."

Daisuke was right. I let my hands fall from my face.

"That's better," Daisuke said, smiling at me. "Now. We need to find out about this ninja."

"Where do we start?" I asked.

"I can speak to the samurai. They'll take me more seriously than you trying to ask them questions. Is there anyone here you can speak to?"

I remembered Emiko. "Yes," I said. "In the kitchens."

Daisuke smiled. "You make friends wherever you go," he said. "Well, good. You go to the kitchens and I'll go to the samurai's quarters. Let's see what we can discover. We'll meet back here at dusk."

I turned to go.

"And Kimi," Daisuke called after me. I looked back at him. "Be careful. Don't draw attention to yourself. This is dangerous." I slid a hand up my sleeve and pulled out the kitchen knife that had not left my side, so that Daisuke could see its blade.

"Don't worry about me," I said.

Emiko wasn't in the kitchen. She wasn't in the laundry either.

"Have you seen Emiko?" I asked a man who was scrubbing bowls. He nodded toward the stable. "Thank you!" I called over my shoulder.

I burst into the stable and froze at the door. Three samurai soldiers were in the small building, turning over boxes and digging among the hay. I tried to back out, unnoticed, but one of the guards swiveled around.

"What are you doing here?" he asked angrily.

I pulled my shoulders back. "Choose your words carefully," I said. "You shouldn't address me like that!" I watched as the soldier scanned my appearance, taking in the luxurious silk of my kimono. His gaze faltered.

"I apologize," he said. "I was startled. Are you lost?"

"No. Even girls from the court know where the

stables are. I like the horses," I said. "I bring them treats sometimes."

One of the soldier's companions strode over toward me. "There has been thieving in the kitchens," he said. "And smuggling of food. It's dangerous here for someone such as yourself." I could smell his sour breath and tried not to shudder in disgust.

As I stepped forward, I heard one of the rafters creak. I glanced up and saw Emiko! She had climbed into the loft of the stables to hide. *She must have been here when the soldiers arrived*, I realized.

"Let me past," I ordered. "I came here to see the horses and that's what I'm going to do." I tried to look up at Emiko without the guards noticing.

Help me, she mouthed. I knew she had to get out of here. And I knew I had to help. I had to distract them somehow.

I turned back into the stable, thinking quickly. "Let me see the rice," I ordered. "My friends at court will love hearing about this little adventure. Stolen rice!" I laughed. "How amusing. Do people really steal such things?"

I heard the quiet whisper of hay as Emiko fell to the ground behind us and knew that she could slip out of the door as long as the soldiers didn't notice her.

Terrified that the soldiers would turn and see my

friend, I tried to pick up the saddlebag, but it was heavier than I expected and I stumbled forward. My wig shifted slightly on my head, but now all the samurai were focused on my struggle with the rice.

"You should leave now," one said. "We have work to do."

They drew their swords and sliced through the hay to see if there was anyone hiding there.

I backed away silently. Then I turned around. No one was there; Emiko had made her escape. I walked out of the stables, my palms sweating, and stepped into the fresh air.

"Halt!" called out a voice. I froze on the spot. One of the samurai strode up to me. He reached out a hand and pulled at my wig. He must have seen it slip when I'd stumbled. My hands flew to my scalp.

"What is this?" he said. "A disguise?"

I tried to laugh scornfully, but the laugh dried up in my throat. "Don't be ridiculous," I said. "I—"

"Silence!" the soldier interrupted. Any respect for a high-ranking girl had disappeared. "I've had enough of you, snooping around. Are you some kind of spy? Or are you the thief in disguise?" He threw the wig in the dirt at my feet and gripped me under the armpit. His fingers tightened around my arm, causing me to cry out. But there was no one to hear, other than the laughing soldiers in the doorway of the stable. The samurai dragged me toward a corner of the compound. "You can stay in the cells until the Administrator is ready to deal with you," he said. I tried to struggle in his grip, but he quickly unsheathed his *tanto* dagger and held it to my throat.

"Any more of that and you'll feel the trickle of your own blood," he snarled. I stopped struggling and surrendered myself as he dragged me toward the cells. I was his prisoner.

If I reached out both my hands, I could touch either side of the room. The packed earth below me smelled of dampness, and the heavy, grilled door of my cell was smeared with grease from the many dirty hands that had grappled uselessly with the lock. I kneeled in the center of the room and tried to meditate. I didn't need to close my eyes—darkness surrounded me. I waited for my heartbeat to slow as I took long, deep breaths. But I couldn't slow my mind; it was racing. I had been locked up here for what felt like hours.

The glow of a lamp lit up the darkness, and heavy shadows moved across the floor of my cell as someone approached. *Thank the gods!* I thought. *Someone has come to get me out of here.* But, no. It was a new guard, here to relieve his compatriot.

The two men grunted to each other, as the person with the lamp took over. He watched his colleague march away, then turned to inspect the girl in the cell behind him. I gasped as I saw Tatsuya's face and I scrambled across the floor to reach out a hand to the lacquered edge of his uniform.

"Tatsuya! Help me!" I said. Tatsuya looked momentarily surprised, but then his face turned cold and he straightened up. He turned his back on me and stood rigidly to attention, his sword glittering in the moonlight.

"I see Hana isn't the only person to have suffered in the fire," he said, his back to me. "Your hair is looking interesting these days." How could he use my injuries to taunt me?

"Please help," I begged. My old friend ignored me. I felt anger firing inside me and I climbed to my feet. I would no longer beg—not to this traitor. I brought my face close to his ear and whispered.

"You've changed, Tatsuya," I said, "and not for the better. You've been corrupted by privilege. Remember when you couldn't even pour a cup of *cha*? Well, I do. I refused to laugh at you back then, but I'm laughing at you now. You're pathetic. If I poured you a cup of tea now, I'd spit in it!"

Tatsuya swirled around and brought his face close to mine, through the grids of the door. "You've no idea what you're talking about," he hissed. "So keep quiet. Unless . . ." I heard a cold hiss as he partly unsheathed his sword. The threat hung in the air between us.

After a moment, he turned away again, but as he turned, I saw that his neck guard had slipped and I caught sight of something in the lamplight. Curved strokes in black ink on white skin.

I shoved a fist in my mouth to stop myself from crying out.

A tattoo!

Tatsuya was the enemy in our midst.

He was the ninja!

CHAPTER TWENTY-TWO

I scrambled back in my cell, just as more lamps emerged, bobbing like glowworms. With a swish of silk, Akane appeared. Her face was illuminated by the golden light. It cast sharp, ugly shadows, and for a moment it was difficult to recognize this woman as the beautiful wife of the Administrator. Mother stood beside her, her face serious.

"Release this girl," Akane snapped at Tatsuya.

As Tatsuya fumbled with the lock, I stepped forward into the light cast by the lamps. My mother gazed at me, her face unreadable, her eyes like dark pools. Then, slowly, she shook her head at me. As the door creaked open and I stepped outside, shame flooded through me.

Akane looked me up and down appraisingly. She raised an eyebrow. "I hadn't expected this from you," she said before turning back to the compound.

Tatsuya followed her, and Mother and I brought up the rear. Guilt scorched my heart as I kept pace.

"How could you?" Mother whispered. I saw her shoulders sag beneath her kimono, and for the first time, she looked old. Akane and Tatsuya had pulled ahead. "This is the most crucial time for our family, and you get yourself thrown into a cell and paraded across the compound without your wig on. When will this end? Why can't you follow Hana's lead and adapt to life here?"

"It wasn't my fault—" I protested, but Mother turned her back on me and walked toward our apartment.

Too many people had turned their backs on me today. I couldn't hold in my frustration. "You don't want to know me anymore, do you?" I asked, my voice hoarse. "I can't help it that my hair is gone and you think I'm ugly."

Mother stopped walking.

"I can't help that I've changed," I shouted back at her, not caring who overheard. "When Father died and you left with Moriyasu, I had to fight for myself."

Slowly she turned to me. I could see tears streak her face, lit golden by the lamp that swung loosely from her hand.

"I have never forgiven myself for what happened that day," she said. "I had to get your brother out, but I never meant to abandon you and Hana. And you're right that I don't know you anymore. My Kimi would never behave like this."

I watched Mother walk away. I wanted to call after her, say I was sorry. Had Mother's heart left me for good? I waited to see if she would pause to look back—just once, just to show she still loved me. But she ducked her head and disappeared inside the building. I was left alone in the dark.

When I got back to our apartment, Moriyasu was in his own room, asleep. Hana and Mother sat on the side of Hana's bed, clearly waiting for me.

Mother threw a weary hand in my direction. "Here she is," she said, before rising and turning into her own room. The door closed behind her with a click. She hadn't even said good night.

Hana stood up and walked over to me. I waited for her to apologize for her angry words earlier in the day; surely she would see that now I was tired and upset. But she raised a hand in the air and struck me, slapping my face hard so that my head jerked around. I put a hand to my mouth, and when I pulled it away, red blood was smeared across my fingertips. I looked back at my sister; I was too shocked for the slap to hurt, but the expression on my sister's face struck at my heart. She pushed me roughly in the chest, sending me staggering back.

"I don't want you near me," she said.

"Stop this!" I cried as Hana gave me another angry shove. With a sob, Hana pushed past me and ran out into the gardens. I waited for my ragged breathing to slow down, and then I followed.

Hana was leaning against the trunk of the maple tree, gazing out over the deserted courtyard. As I came up behind her, she turned so that I could see her profile lit by the light of the moon.

"I'm sorry if I've brought you unhappiness," I said quietly. Hana didn't react, so I plunged on. "But there's something you must know. Tatsuya is the ninja. He was guarding me in the cell and I saw his tattoo." I waited for Hana to say something.

"So now you add lying to your list of achievements," she said bitterly. "Well done, Kimi. You must be really proud of yourself."

I could not believe my sister was saying this to me. I grabbed her shoulders and forced her around to look me in the face. "How can you say that?"

Hana looked away.

"Look at me!" I demanded.

Hana lifted her eyes and met my gaze. "I can't believe it," she said. "I won't."

"You have to," I said. "It's the truth."

Hana pulled herself from me and backed away among the leaves of the maple tree. Her voice was weak. "But he's always hated the ninja—they took his father. He wouldn't become one of them! You must be confused, Kimi."

"I'm sure there is a good reason," I said gently, "and I admit that I don't know what it is yet. But there's no escaping what I saw tonight. Tatsuya wears the tattoo of the ninja. He does. Something has happened to him—and something is waiting to happen. We cannot stand aside and watch."

I held out my fingertips to Hana, in our secret signal of kinship. After a moment's hesitation, she brought her own fingertips against mine. She was starting to forgive me, and I hoped that she would also begin hearing the truth of what I was saying.

Hana gazed up at the moon, milky white in the night sky. "It's the Shogun's meeting tomorrow," she muttered. "We had better rest."

Sighing deeply, I followed my sister back to our beds. She was right. Tomorrow would be a long day and I would need all my energy. I only hoped that Daisuke would stand by my side. After today, I wasn't sure who else I could count on.

Mother woke us early the next morning.

"We must look our best for the meeting," she explained. "It is crucial to make an impression if we are to persuade the clans." Meekly I allowed Mother to hold kimonos up in front of me until she gave a sharp nod.

"Yes, this one," she said. Even I had to admit, it was beautiful. The silk was of the same pale pink as a cherry blossom and the undergarment was a vibrant green, just like the sticky buds of spring. My obi sash was embroidered in emerald, against a deeper pink. Mother brought the folds of the robes around my body, pulling and adjusting, until the hem hung at just the right length.

As she pulled the wig on my head—rescued from the stables—she looked at me properly for the first time that morning.

"I do not think you are ugly," she said. "You are my beautiful daughter. But this is your life now, Kimi." She pulled me into an embrace and I knew I still had her love.

"Do not worry," I said. "When Moriyasu is *Jito*, I will always make myself presentable. I will not let the family down."

Mother smiled uncertainly. "Why the change of heart?" she asked.

"Last night I found myself in a cell—and I saw how much I'd upset you and Hana," I explained. "It was never what I set out to achieve. And now, as you have said, we have to show brave faces to the world. We need to be united."

Mother hesitated; then she nodded her head in acknowledgment.

"This is more than I could have hoped for," she said. "I look forward to watching you and your sister and brother care for the estates. Thank you."

The door slid open. Hana stood in the doorway, panting. Then she raced over and grabbed my hand. "Come on!" she said, pulling me after her.

"Girls!" Mother cried out, startled. "Where are you going? The meeting—" But it was too late. We were already racing down the walkway.

Hana dragged me behind her until we arrived at the door of the samurai's quarters.

"What are you doing?" I asked. "What's happening?"

Hana tried to catch her breath. "I can't stand it anymore," she said. "I couldn't sleep last night thinking about it. I have to know! I have to hear it from Tatsuya!"

Soldiers were all over the compound, making sure it was secure for the day's meeting. The head of every important clan would be there.

As we made our way across the gravel, no one turned to look at us. *We fit in*, I thought to myself. *No one stares at us anymore.* I watched Hana as she walked ahead of me, keeping her steps small and meek, despite her urgency. Her kimono billowed heavily in the breeze as she peered into soldiers' faces, looking for our friend.

We found Tatsuya in a secluded corner of the pool garden, hidden by the drooping leaves of the willow tree. This was where we had first sat with him and where he had first turned on us. He swiveled around at the sound of our approach, and his face turned pale.

"What's going on?" I asked. There was no time for polite civilities now.

Tatsuya looked past us, desperate to escape. But Hana and I stood shoulder to shoulder.

"I don't know what you're talking about," he said. "Let me past. I have work to do."

"What work?" I challenged. "An assassination?" I watched the blood drain from his face. My guess was right. "After all, isn't that what ninja are sent to do? Assassinate?"

I heard Hana gasp in disbelief beside me. "Tell us it's not true," she said, reaching out a hand. "Tatsuya, tell us it can't be."

Tatsuya raised a trembling hand toward Hana's. Then his face contorted with aggression and he grabbed her wrist, twisting it behind her back so that she was forced to collapse to the mossy ground with a cry of pain. A corner of her kimono draped in the pond, soaking up water that turned her rose-colored kimono a deep red—the color of blood. Tatsuya pushed past her, but I threw myself in front of him and punched him straight in the gut. He staggered but then brought his own hand around to chop my neck. I was flung forward, facedown in the dirt. Tatsuya didn't hesitate. I turned to see him pulling his curved sword out of its hilt; with his other hand he dragged Hana up from the ground by her hair. He pinned her against his chest and held the silver blade of his sword to the pale skin of her neck.

"No!" I cried. I pulled the kitchen knife out of my sleeve and leaped forward, pressing its point against the quick pulse in the base of Tatsuya's throat. I watched a trickle of blood score a path down his chest. "One more move and I kill you," I hissed between gritted teeth. "I promise you that."

Tatsuya's eyes looked wild as he stared back at me. I could hear Hana quietly sobbing. Thoughts raced through my mind as time stood still. *Could Tatsuya really be capable of killing Hana? Was I capable of plunging my knife into the flesh of my old friend?* I couldn't understand what had brought Tatsuya to these desperate actions. Then Tatsuya's face crumbled. He let the sword drop to the ground, and Hana staggered to one side as he fell to his knees. I stepped away and he leaned forward so that his forehead pressed against the moss. I could see his sides heaving. Then he sat back on his haunches and lifted his face to the sky, exposing the snow-white skin of his throat. The ninja

251

tattoo was there for all to see now.

"Kill me," he said. He looked at the knife gripped in my fist and I could see that the glint in his eyes had turned dull. "I'm already dead."

CHAPTER TWENTY-THREE

Hana rushed to Tatsuya's side.

"We could not kill you," she told him, placing a hand on his arm. "And you're *not* dead." Hana looked up at me, her eyes pleading with me to forgive Tatsuya. *How can she be so good?* I thought. *A moment ago, this boy was pressing death against her throat and now she's comforting him?*

I kneeled down beside the two of them. Tatsuya looked up at me, his eyes streaming.

"I'm sorry," he said. I could see that his spirit had broken. Who was I to make him feel any worse? I reached out a hand and rescued his sword from the ground.

"You'd better put this back in its sheath," I said, handing it to him. "Tell us what's happened to you." In the distance, we could hear people call out to each other in greeting as they collected for the Shogun's meeting. We didn't have much time. "Who are you here to kill?"

Tatsuya looked across the garden, toward the main part of the compound.

"The Shogun," he said dully. "Tonight."

I gave a start and Hana flinched back.

"Oh, Tatsuya," I said. "Why?"

Tatsuya looked down at his hands and rubbed them together, trying to encourage blood into the deathly white fingertips. "I knew who it was, coming after me . . . when I was kidnapped by the ninja," he said. Hana and I exchanged a confused glance. "You see, I was lying to you even back in Master Goku's school." He stood up and walked a step away. "I have always been a liar," he said bitterly. He turned around to face us. "I don't deserve your friendship. I never have! My father . . . my father is a ninja leader and when those men snatched me away, they were taking me back to him. I bet you can hardly bear to look at me now, can you?"

Hana got to her feet and walked over to him. She rested a hand against the side of his face. "Tell us the rest of your story," she prompted.

"My father sent me here to kill the Shogun," said Tatsuya. "If I did that, he said, I could be released from the brotherhood of the ninja. I would be left alone to forge my own path in life. Of course, this freedom would come with a price—I would have to live with another man's blood on my hands."

"A good man's blood on your hands," I interrupted.

Tatsuya nodded. "A good man's blood." He threw a desperate glance at Hana and me. "I thought I could do it. Thought I could harden my heart. Until . . ." He gazed at Hana and affection flooded his eyes. "Until you two arrived. Just the sight of your faces brought so many memories back. Memories of honor and training, codes of conduct, of Goku . . . That's why I couldn't bear to be around either of you. It was too painful, knowing what I had to do." Tatsuya sank back onto the bench.

"You don't have to do this," I said quietly. "You have a choice. Look at the Shogun—such an honorable man. He does not deserve death. You would never be able to forgive yourself if you killed him. Would you?"

Tatsuya gave a hollow, bitter laugh. He gazed over the walls of the Shogun's compound toward the forest beyond, a hiding place for so many secrets.

"Perhaps that's what my father wanted," he said. He drove a fist into his open palm. "How could I have been so stupid? Father knew I would be tormented for the rest of my life by such an assassination. That was part of his plan, part of his revenge for me not wanting to join him as a ninja from the beginning. He wants me to live a life of misery." Tatsuya's eyes narrowed with anger. "Oh, my father is an excellent ninja. He can kill a person without using a sword or a knife. He can kill their soul."

A gong rang out, calling people to the Shogun's meeting. Its sound reverberated in the air between us.

"We have to go," I said, getting to my feet. "We won't say a word. But, Tatsuya—you must not do anything rash. Don't go ahead with the assassination—promise me."

Tatsuya nodded. "I promise," he said weakly.

But I wasn't convinced. Something awful had happened to our friend. He could see no way out. What if he did something desperate? Another urgent peal of bells rang out.

"Hana," I said gently, letting my sister know that we had to go. The fate of our family was waiting for us in the Shogun's meeting room. We strode out of the garden, Tatsuya leading the way. But an uncomfortable question kept hammering away in my head. Someone had commissioned the ninja to kill the Shogun—why else would Tatsuya's father ask his son to assassinate this man?

Is this another part of Uncle's plan? I wondered. If he was sending ninja into the Shogun's compound, it could mean only one thing. He really was after the greatest prize of all—the title of Shogun.

Mother was waiting for us with Moriyasu. He looked very grown up in his outfit and his cheeks shone from the cold water he had splashed over his face.

"There you are," said Mother. "Where have you been? What's happened to your clothes?" Hana and I hurriedly brushed the dirt from our kimonos.

"Kimi tripped and I helped her up," Hana explained, shrugging her shoulders. Fortunately there wasn't time for Mother to question us further.

As we stepped into the hall, I gasped. Low wooden tables were ranged around the edges of the room, and at the tables kneeled more lords and councillors than I had ever seen at my father's gatherings. These were the men who would decide our fate. They were resplendent in their outfits of silk and brocade. Their hair was well oiled and scraped back. Some of the men wore stiff *eboshi* caps; each wore the *mon* of their family. A blind *biwa* player sat in a corner, plucking at his lute until the meeting was ready to begin. The scent of wood sorrel filled the air, and through the sliding screens, the play of light in the garden cast shadows over the men's faces, though nothing could disguise how serious they looked.

Hana came to stand beside me. "It's impressive," she said. Her voice trembled.

"Let's hope we impress them back," I replied.

Mother walked ahead of us, her hand on Moriyasu's shoulder, and I stepped forward to follow. But I heard my name sound out behind me, and when I glanced around I saw my friend Emiko peeking from behind a sliding door. She waved a hand at me, urging me to join her. I glanced hesitantly back into the main hall. Hana was frowning at me, waiting for me to follow.

"You go ahead," I said. "I'll catch up." Then I ducked behind the sliding door.

"I'm sorry to disturb you," Emiko said. She twisted a dirty cloth between her hands, and I tried not to notice how shabby her clothes looked. Councillors cast us curious glances as they walked past into the main hall.

"What is it?" I asked. "Is everything all right?" I knew Emiko had to have a good reason for drawing attention to herself in this way.

"I wanted to thank you for helping me in the stable," she said. "And I'm sorry that you were thrown into a cell. I would never have willingly brought such dishonor upon you. I haven't been able to sleep for the guilt."

I laughed. "Is that all?" I asked. I wondered if I should tell Emiko about all the situations I'd already been in—sleeping in an inn full of drunks, hiding beneath floorboards, disguising myself as a boy, and climbing among trees. A few hours in a cell had been nothing! But as I looked down at my silk kimono, I wondered if she would believe me. I shook my head. "Go back to the kitchen," I whispered. "I don't want you getting caught. You still have a lot of people to feed outside these walls, remember?"

Emiko's face flushed with gratitude. "Okay." She nodded. "Thanks for everything, Kimi. Oh—and one other thing. I've heard that some of the powerful families here have been speaking out against your plight. But don't worry, the servants tell me that many more families speak up for you. Now is your time!" Then she ran down the walkway, back to the clouds of steam in the kitchen.

"I hope so," I said to myself as I watched her disappear.

I stepped back into the main hall. The Shogun and his mother sat on the raised platform, in front of a painted screen. The Shogun looked composed and sure of himself. Had he already made up his mind about what to do? I felt my throat go dry at the thought of what lay ahead.

"Remember what I said," hissed a voice to my left. I paused and noticed that from behind a lacquered screen poked the edge of a peacock-blue kimono. I looked around me, but all attention was on the Shogun. I stepped to one side and leaned back so that I could see behind the screen.

It was Akane, with Tatsuya. What were they doing? I felt the hairs stiffen on the back of my neck and I drew closer.

"I can't," said Tatsuya. "I refuse!" I could see that he was doing his best to be brave, but his voice trembled.

"You have no choice!" Akane said. She brought her face close to Tatsuya's and her features distorted as she narrowed her eyes and sneered. *How did I ever think she was beautiful?* I thought. "You must complete your mission by the end of this meeting," Akane continued, "or I promise you I will complete it for you—and put an end to *your* life, too. Don't forget, little one, I have more fatal knowledge in my little finger than has ever filled your empty head. I could crush you like that!" And she snapped her fingers in his face.

It hit me instantly. How could I have been a fool for so long? I had admired her strength and poise, but this woman was the evil at the heart of the Shogun's compound.

As she turned to slip out from behind the lacquered screen, I stepped boldly forward, as if I had been doing nothing other than walking confidently into the hall. I bowed my head at Akane as she passed and she flashed me an insincere smile. But as she walked in front of me, I noticed the arch of her neck and the flash of white behind her ear. There, I saw the sign of death. It was the ninja tattoo, kept hidden for so long by the thick swathes of her hair. She was another ninja!

I stepped into the hall, my heart racing. Akane took her place next to her powerful husband, and I knew there was nothing I could say or do. The meeting had begun. I remembered what Akane had told me over that game of Go—timing was everything. My hands bunched into fists beneath the sleeves of my kimono. I would not be a helpless bystander; I would bide my time.

And when the time was right, I would know what to do.

CHAPTER TWENTY-FOUR

I took my place beside my mother. Across from us sat Daisuke and the monks. Each of them wore prayer beads and their heads were closely shaved. The folds of their robes hid the panels of their armor, but their swords were by their sides. Daisuke looked across the room and I smiled. Even though my senses were drawn tight, it was good to see a friend. I ached to race across the room and tell him everything I had seen and heard, but we were surrounded by councillors. Now was not the time.

The Shogun raised a hand and the *biwa* player fell silent. "I have come to a decision," he said, addressing the room. He did not raise his voice, but he did not have to—we were all listening keenly. Beside him, his mother gazed down at her lap, her face unreadable. "But before I tell you my thoughts, I would like to hear what the clans have decided." He nodded his head at the Administrator.

"I speak only for the greater good of my fellows," the

Administrator said. He stood tall and looked proud. It made my hackles rise. He swirled around and cast a dismissive hand in the direction of my brother. I was proud to see that Moriyasu did not flinch. "This *boy* is no leader of men. Hidehira has proved himself to have the skill and leadership to inspire."

I bit my lip to stop myself from crying out. Inspire? My uncle had not inspired anything but fear and intimidation; surely everyone knew that. I cast a startled glance at Mother, and she shook her head. I knew there was nothing I could say. I had to sit here and listen to these words, hollow of any true meaning. But there was no trace now of the kindness he'd shown on his wedding day.

The Administrator continued talking as the councillors listened respectfully. "In less than four moons Hidehira has converged several estates." *Converged?* I thought. *Or attacked?* "This vigor is impressive. It's enough to persuade me to stand by Hidehira's side. Moriyasu is still a boy, preoccupied with games. My wife has told me about his endless games of Go!" He ended with a sneer.

Men and their wives in the room chortled. I glanced at Akane in her blue silk—the color of a strutting, posturing peacock—the color of deceit. She gazed straight ahead, batting a fan before her face. The fan was painted with the pattern of peacock feathers and they shifted between different shades of blue as the silk of the fan moved through the air. For a moment, it was mesmerizing. But then I looked past the fan at Akane's eyes and saw there the cold glitter of a deadly foe. She had never cared for our family, I realized. She only wanted us close so that she could keep a careful eye on us, and we had been fool enough to accept the embrace. She smiled at the Administrator and for a moment I suppressed the urge to throw myself at her, scratching the smile from her face.

It was Daisuke's turn to speak. His robes glowed in the light and gave him a quality that made him look as though he were from another world. He looked around the room, taking all of us in one by one. The Administrator sat stiffly as we all waited for Daisuke to begin.

Daisuke raised a hand at an open window. "Out there, people are starving," he said. "Villagers have no food, communities are plagued by sickness, and innocent people dare not sleep in their beds for fear of attack. I have nursed the sick and dying under my master, but I have never seen devastation like this. Soon, even you"—he shot out a hand at the Shogun—"may feel the impact of Lord Steward Yamamoto." People around the room gasped. "But this doesn't have to happen. Not if we fight back together. Moriyasu comes from a lineage of honor and respect. Let those qualities live on in our people. Let Moriyasu take his rightful place as *Jito*, and we will save thousands of lives."

I looked at the Shogun. Daisuke's speech had been a dangerous one. People talked urgently among themselves, discussing what Daisuke had said. Frightened that opinion was turning against my friend, I looked over at him. But he remained calm and serene.

Someone else raised a hand, requesting permission to speak.

"Oh no," I whispered to Hana. It was the older woman who had done so much to offend my mother and our family with her rude remarks. She would surely speak out against Moriyasu. I looked at my brother; his face had turned pale.

The woman bowed respectfully to the Shogun and then to the Shogun's mother. Then she nodded stiffly in the direction of our mother.

"This woman came to court a widow," she said. "And I could not understand why a widow would travel through the countryside, without her husband to protect her. To my mind, it was a scandal. It broke every rule. . . ." She paused and I felt my throat constrict as I waited to hear what she would say next. "But I was wrong." I saw the way her lip trembled, as she struggled to contain her emotions. "I, too, have a family. And to see this woman's composure and grace, after so much has happened to her, is a lesson to us all. It is surely a lesson her children have already learned under her example. I stand for Moriyasu and pledge my clan behind his cause!"

The voices in the room sounded out even louder. This was becoming a debate beyond anything I expected. This was no longer just about the right thing to do, the proper thing to do—I could see that people's hearts were being touched. All because my mother had behaved well in court and impressed her peers. Her strategy had worked, after all. Her gentle, polite behavior had done more than my angry casting about. It had won us friends.

"I am sorry I didn't listen to you," I whispered to Mother. She nodded her head in acknowledgment, then bowed once to the woman who spoke up for us.

"Thank you," Mother said. She turned to the room at large. "Thank you to all of you. I know you will make the right decision." Two spots of red appeared on her cheeks. She knew as well as I that our lives were in the hands of these people. "My children are more than capable of carrying on my husband's legacy. They have made me very proud. I know they will continue to fill me with pride. They are the light of my lives; they could light the way for the province, too. I only hope that you allow them to shine."

"Enough!" interrupted the Shogun. He stood up, his silk robes shifting over his limbs. Nervously I glanced around the room. Where was Tatsuya? Did the Shogun have any idea that people were planning his death? "My decision is confirmed by everything I have heard. I shall strip Hidehira of his *Jito* title and pass the stewardship to Moriyasu." My brother's face flushed with pleasure and he straightened his back, as he gazed around the room, nodding his head in thanks to the councillors. "And I will support the monks in their push against Hidehira. We will fight by their side. This meeting is over. You may depart."

People climbed to their feet and huddled in groups, talking low and fast. Some men strode out of the room in disgust.

"There will be war," one of them commented to a neighbor. "This is a disaster."

Other people gathered around our family to congratulate us. I pushed my way through the crowd to see the Shogun helping his mother to her feet. The Administrator was also up on the platform and whispered furiously to the Shogun until I saw his mother silence the man with a short, angry remark.

Beyond the crowds, I spotted Akane. She was motioning to someone. My eyes traveled across the room, but I already knew who I would see in the doorway.

Tatsuya.

The moments slowed as I watched. I saw the way that Tatsuya's face contorted with indecision. His eyes came around to meet mine, and as we shared a long glance, I knew with deadly certainty that Tatsuya was near to breaking his promise. He wasn't strong enough; Akane had won.

When I looked back around, Akane was watching me, her face frozen. *She knows that I've uncovered her secret,* I realized. She had seen the shared glance between Tatsuya and me. I watched as Hana went over to speak to Tatsuya. Had she seen the same things I'd noticed? Perhaps she was going to persuade him to stay strong. If only I could do something to stop what was unraveling. I took a step toward the Administrator's wife.

"There's a killer in our midst!" Akane called out angrily. She pointed at Tatsuya, who was still in the doorway. I had never seen anyone look *less* like an assassin. Tatsuya's eyes widened, and Hana looked around in alarm.

"That soldier!" Akane went on. "Arrest him! I have just found out on good authority that he is planning to kill the Shogun. Look on his neck—you'll see the sign of the ninja."

"No!" Tatsuya called out. Hana flung herself in front of him protectively, but it was no use. The soldiers surrounded him and dragged him away, and I heard my friend's cries echo off the walls. I looked back around at Akane, and she cast me a superior, jubilant glance.

I've won, she mouthed at me. Then she began to walk out of the hall. I was watching evil turn its back on me. I would not let this happen. Ninjas had already escaped me once at the monastery and again at the compound.

I would not let it happen again.

CHAPTER TWENTY-FIVE

S top!" I called out.
  The hall fell silent. Akane froze and turned around to look at me, disbelieving. "How dare you speak to me like that," she said threateningly. She started to run toward me, but then remembered herself, casting nervous glances around at the onlookers. She tried to smile, but the smile slid off of her face. "You are a mere child," she said more gently. "You may not speak to me like that." The Shogun had climbed down off his platform and stood by my side. He was looking closely at Akane. Her face flushed red as she realized that the whole court was watching her.

"This woman is a ninja," I said, turning to the Shogun. "Look behind her ear, you'll see for yourself." The Shogun hesitated. Akane started to back out of the room, but the Shogun gave a sharp nod to the samurai at the door and they came to stand on either side of her, the light glancing off their red-lacquered armor. She did not dare move.

"Inspect her," the Shogun said.

"No!" Akane cried out. The soldiers gripped each of her arms and held her steady as the Shogun's mother approached. Her mouth turned down at the corners as she yanked Akane's coils of ebony hair to one side.

"There," the Shogun's mother said. "I always sensed this one was not to be trusted." No one moved. We could all see the black, fluid strokes of the tattoo—the permanent mark of a silent assassin.

"How could you?" asked a solitary voice. It was the Administrator. He stepped up to his wife, gazing into her eyes. Her eyes glittered back ferociously. Then she pulled her head back and spat in her husband's face. Women cried out and the Shogun's mother hissed through her teeth in disgust.

The reaction of the crowd was distraction enough. Akane tore her arms free of the guards' grip and wheeled around. She leaped into the air and fiercely kicked her heels into their chests. As they staggered back, she landed and immediately ran toward them, delivering another flying kick at the nearest. He fell back onto his companion and they skidded across the polished floor.

The Shogun called out for more guards.

"Seize her!" he cried as they entered the room, their swords already unsheathed and glittering in the light. Akane backed away, laughing breathlessly.

"You can lock that boy up, but I am the *real* assassin!" She pulled her fan out from her sleeve and gave it an angry flick that snapped it open. Then she gave the fan a second flick and with a snap, sharp, pointed metal teeth appeared from the prongs of the fan.

The soldiers hesitated, glancing nervously at the Shogun. Akane arched the fan. The metal of those deadly points shone. Then she whipped around and threw the fan at a screened window. It tore through the screen and circled back to her waiting grasp. She pointed the fan across the room, at a boy who had been watching silently all this time.

At my brother.

"No!" I cried out. I sprang toward her, but Akane pulled her arm back and hurled the fan so that it sliced through the air. Moriyasu stood against the wall, his face blank with shock, his body unmoving. The fan hissed as it tore across the room.

A body arched through the air. Amber silk shone in the sun as a woman threw herself in front of Moriyasu.

"Mother!" Hana cried out.

The fan thudded home, driving its spikes into our mother's chest. Red blood stained the front of the amber kimono as she fell to her knees. Moriyasu whimpered at her side. Gone was the brave boy who

272

would be *Jito*. In his place was a child who had seen his parent wounded. Mother's eyes rolled back in her head as Moriyasu tried to cradle her. I felt my heart freeze over.

Akane's laughter, shrill and evil, brought me back to my senses. Guards tried to overpower her, but she was too skilled. The samurai didn't stand a chance; with deadly accuracy she attacked. Her hands whirled in a series of double punches and she leaped into the air again and again to send out fierce kicks, spinning to meet new attackers before they could assemble their onslaught.

Then she threw her hands onto the floor and cartwheeled through the soldiers, moving so quickly that each attempt to catch her left the soldiers' hands closing on empty air.

Akane scowled back at her missed target and ran toward the doors of the hall, her blue silk kimono billowing. Her hair had come loose, and as it streamed behind her, the ninja tattoo shone out vividly. I grabbed a porcelain vase and hurled it at her. It crashed into a pillar near her head.

"You!" she hissed. She grabbed a sword from a soldier in pursuit and threw him into another soldier. Then the two of us stood face-to-face before the main doors of the meeting room. "Prepare to die!"

I yanked a sword from a startled nobleman as

Akane lunged forward and brought it up to meet her attack, deflecting the blade from my body. Akane lifted her sword above her head and sliced down toward my heart. I moved out of range just in time, feeling a *whoosh* of air across my chest.

Akane sliced hard from the left. There was a clash of steel as I stepped into her and brought my sword down the length of her blade until it jammed into hers at the hilt. We stood in a deadlock, swords pushing against each other, my eyes never leaving my enemy's.

"Murderer!" I hissed.

Her lips curled in a sneer. "Peasant!" she threw back. She couldn't have known that this was the best thing for her to say. My cousin Ken-ichi had once tried to wound me with that very word—it hadn't worked then, either. I had spent my days among the peasants of this province and they had sheltered me. I was proud to be called a peasant; proud enough to keep fighting. New energy pulsed through my veins and the fight began again.

As Akane and I fought, people ran from the room. I was vaguely aware of Daisuke by my mother's side, but I had to keep my every thought for the fight in hand. Akane began to tire. I could see that her lunges were slower and her blocks less accurate. Her life of luxury had taken its toll. *I'm winning!* I thought as a finger of sweat trickled down my back beneath my kimono. *If I can just keep going.*

I pushed Akane back against a screened window. As she backed away, swinging her sword wildly, her foot caught on the hem of her kimono and she staggered against the frame. I bounded forward and brought the blade of my sword against her throat. I leaned my weight into it and pressed down against her skin. Akane was panting hard from the exertions. But my enemy's gaze never faltered, even as blood poured down her neck from the wound to her cheek.

"Your day is done," I told her.

With a quick movement, she snatched a hand toward the sleeve of her robe and threw a twist of paper to the floor. A loud popping sound, like instant thunder, hurt my ears and suddenly black smoke filled my eyes and mouth, making me cough and choke.

Akane took a step up onto my knee and then onto my shoulder. With a mocking laugh, she jumped from one man's shoulder to another soldier's head. Before people had a chance to realize what was happening, she was leaping across the room, using those gathered for the meeting as her stepping-stones. Coughing and retching, I watched as she launched herself into the air and dived through an open window, her body arching. But her kimono caught on the frame. She fiercely tried to tug herself free, as I climbed to my feet. She glanced back up at me, desperation filling her face.

My enemy was trapped and she would feel the sting of my blade. I ran across the room, intent on vengeance, determined to see the pain of death etched across Akane's face.

"Kimi!" My sister was cradling our mother's head to her chest as she called out to me, her voice tortured by sobs.

"She's still alive," Moriyasu said. From behind him, Daisuke watched to see what I would do next.

The sword clattered to the polished floor. I ran across the bloody boards to Mother's side. Her pale hand languished on the cold tiles and I lifted it to hold between my own bloodied fingers. My mother's eyes fluttered and flickered open. She smiled, sending another thin stream of blood falling from the corner of her mouth, down her cheek, and to the tiled floor.

"I am so proud of you all," she said weakly, her breath wheezing in her chest. "My brave children. Stay strong." Then her face contorted in pain and she coughed. More blood foamed out of her mouth and spread across her cheeks, staining her beautiful face.

"No!" I cried. Hana's body was wracked with sobs.

Moriyasu watched, his face solemn and unmoving, the shock freezing his limbs.

Mother's eyes closed for the final time, like butterflies closing their wings. All three of us watched as the rise and fall of her chest slowed and then ceased. I put Mother's hand back down on her chest, beside her heart. Then I stood up. My sister sobbed quietly at my feet; Moriyasu watched me with wide eyes. Only Daisuke made a move toward me, but I turned away and walked over to the window through which Akane had made her escape.

I gazed out over the rolling hills beyond the compound's walls. My country. As I looked, a bird came to land beside the water of the pond garden. It folded its wings and sang. But its song did not touch my heart. Tears rolled down my cheeks, unchecked. *How much more?* I silently asked the sky. *Shall you tear my heart in two?*

I turned back to look at my sister and brother.

Daisuke arranged our mother's body and cleaned the blood from her skin. Moriyasu came to stand on one side of me, and Hana walked to my other side.

"It's up to us now," I said, retrieving the sword from the floor. Its blade glittered in the light. "Only us."

EPILOGUE

With my mother's last breath, something inside of me died. But more bloodshed lay ahead of us. Uncle Hidehira would not give up; he would fight on. I had made the right decision that day, to turn my back on revenge—to allow Akane to escape. Daisuke had urged me to find the true path, to listen to my heart over anything else. I needed friends like never before. I needed their strength if I was to carry on and find justice. Because without justice this suffering would count for nothing.

Without it, this suffering would become too much for my heart to bear. . . .